MEANT TO BE
TURNING TIDES SERIES BOOK 2

CARLY GRANT

Copyright © 2021 by Carly Grant

All rights reserved.

No part of this book may be reproduced, duplicated, or transmitted in any form or by any electronic or mechanical means, including information storage and retrieval systems without written permission of the author, except for the use of brief quotations in a book review.

This book is a work of fiction. Unless otherwise indicated, all of the names, characters, businesses, places, events and incidents in this book are either the product of the author's imagination or used in a fictitious manner. Any resemblance to persons, living or dead, or places, events or locations is purely coincidental.

MEANT TO BE

A Turning Tides Novel

Welcome to Crestpoint Beach, where warm sands and sea breezes bring sweet second chances, renewed family ties, and the comfort of coming home.

Hannah Taylor is spontaneous and fun. Building contractor Gabe Lawson is all business, a handsome newcomer to Crestpoint Beach who's looking for a fresh start. When Hannah and her sister hire Gabe to help get their beach house B&B inspection-ready ahead of the summer tourist season, sparks fly between these total opposites.

But there's more to both of them than meets the eye, and soon free-spirited Hannah and "measure twice, cut once" Gabe are fighting deeper feelings for each other. When a setback threatens to pull them apart, can Hannah and Gabe turn their "opposites attract" romance into happily-ever-after?

Meant to Be is a clean contemporary romance. Book 2 of the Turning Tides B&B series.

Watch for Book 3, **Maybe This Time**, coming in April 2021.

CHAPTER 1

Crisp footsteps thumped against the wood floor as Crestpoint Beach's local inspector, Jane Peavey, accompanied Hannah Taylor and her sister, Annie, through their grand old Victorian beach house, clipboard in hand.

Hannah anxiously trailed the woman, finding her impossible to read. The inspection had been going on for more than half an hour, but it felt like an eternity as Ms. Peavey strode from one room to the next in her gray pantsuit and low heels, her dark hair pinned into a tight bun on top of her head.

She paused to jot another note on her report, then peered at the sisters over the lenses of her red-framed glasses. "How soon did you say you were planning to open for business?"

Hannah glanced at her older sister. "Hopefully before Memorial Day in a couple of months, right?"

Annie nodded. "At the latest. We'd like to make the most of the summer tourist season."

"Hm," the inspector responded, returning her attention to her report to make yet another notation.

Hannah shot a worried look at Annie. In order for the

beach house to be licensed as a bed-and-breakfast it had to pass a checklist of requirements. They had already been approved for zoning, food service, and sanitation. All that remained was the safety and lodging inspection taking place today. Hannah had hoped they would clear this final hurdle as easily as they had the others, but with every scrape of the inspector's pen across the report on her clipboard, some of that hope began to fade.

"This house originally belonged to our grandparents," she told the woman, trying to make conversation as they headed back downstairs after reviewing the three bedrooms on the second floor. "Annie and I spent some of the best days of our childhoods right outside on that veranda sipping lemonade with our grandma or playing on the beach. We can't wait for our guests to make family memories of their own when they come to stay here."

"Of course." Ms. Peavey's smile stretched thinly on her lips as she paused at the bottom of the staircase. "I believe you mentioned there are more bedrooms on this main level?"

"Two bedrooms and a shared bath," Annie said, indicating their direction and giving Hannah a fatigued look as the inspector marched ahead of them.

They waited in the hallway as Ms. Peavey entered the large bedroom and took out her tape measure. After measuring doorways and floor space around the bed, she moved on to inspect the windows and a dozen other little things before she added even more ink to the paper on her clipboard.

"Does the owner of the house live in the residence full-time?" she asked while she scribbled on her report.

"Yes," Hannah replied. "Annie owns the house along with our dad and me. She's living on the third floor."

The woman's dark eyes flicked over the tops of her glasses

again. "And will that continue to be the case once you're taking in lodgers?"

Annie nodded. "Yes. Why do you ask?"

Ms. Peavey gave them a tight smile. "ADA regulations. Since you'll be owner-occupied during business operations, you don't have to worry about any of those concerns."

Although it was a relief to hear there was something the inspector would not be writing down on her report, Hannah and Annie had already discussed privately that they planned to make one of the first-floor bedrooms and the main bathroom accessible for guests who were unable to stay upstairs. They didn't want to exclude anyone from being able to enjoy the house and its relaxing location.

"All right, I believe I have everything I need," Ms. Peavey said with a sigh. Tucking her pen above her ear, she unclipped her report and held it out to Hannah and Annie.

As curious as Hannah was to see it, she let her sister take the report from the inspector. They read it in silence together, and Hannah couldn't help the feeling of deflation that settled over her.

"Wow, that's a lot of ink. There must be close to twenty things on here that we need to fix or update."

Without commenting, Ms. Peavey slipped her clipboard into the large tote bag on her shoulder and stepped out to the living room with them. "I'll be happy to return for a second look whenever you're ready. Bear in mind, if you do intend to open before the holiday, I wouldn't wait too long to call me back. My schedule fills up quite quickly this time of year."

"We understand," Annie replied, handing the report to Hannah. "Thank you for taking the time to come out. We'll be in touch as soon as possible."

Ms. Peavey shook their hands and said goodbye, then

Annie walked her to the door leading out to the beach. As she departed the house, the inspector's heels clopped down the old veranda's wooden steps.

Just one of the many items in need of repair before they could open for business, according to the list Hannah stared at in disappointment.

Annie came back inside and dropped onto the sofa. "Well, that didn't exactly go as smoothly as we anticipated, did it?"

Hannah sat down next to her, determined to find the bright side. "The list is longer than we hoped, but it's not that bad, actually." She scanned the list and read off a few of the items in need of attention. "Fire alarms and a sprinkler system throughout the house, new locks for all of the guest rooms and exterior entries, a new handrail and taller balusters for the stairs to bring it up to code, some repair work on the veranda steps and railing…"

Annie swiveled a dubious look at her. "It's a lot."

Hannah sighed. "Okay, it's a lot. But we can do this, right?"

She couldn't deny the tug of discouragement that weighed her down, but she refused to give in to it. Turning their grandparents' beautiful old house into a bed-and-breakfast had been her idea initially, a project for her to work on with Annie after her sister's return to Crestpoint Beach a couple of months ago.

Annie had been dealing with the tragic loss of her husband, Derek, a situation complicated even more by her reunion with Noah Davis, the man Hannah's sister had loved since she was in grade school. Living in the beach house had given Annie some much needed space and privacy while she coped with starting over back in the hometown.

For Hannah, working together on the B&B project with Annie had been a chance to reconnect with the sister she adored. They had always been close growing up, even if Hannah sometimes felt a bit overshadowed by her older sister's ambition and success. While Annie had gone off to college in Texas on a scholarship to pursue her career in interior design, Hannah had been content to remain in the hometown with their father all these years.

At the age of thirty, five years younger than Annie, Hannah made a humble, yet comfortable living working at the local gift shop and crafting seashell art. Maybe in a different world she might have had the courage to dream of bigger things, but she was far from unhappy right where she was. Life was pretty great, and it had only gotten better since her sister had come back home.

The bed-and-breakfast was a dream she and Annie shared now, and Hannah was determined to make it work no matter what it took.

"We have several weeks to get everything done and then schedule another inspection, so let's hire some help," she suggested, trying to sound more confident about the idea than she felt.

Finding reputable builders who weren't already booked out months in advance was hard enough in a small tourist town like Crestpoint Beach, but it would be even harder with the summer season coming up fast.

Never mind the fact that their list of beach house fixes, while daunting to Hannah and Annie, was far from the lucrative projects that most contractors would be looking to land.

Still, she pasted on a reassuring smile and patted Annie's shoulder. "One good thing about living in the hometown all my life is that I know practically everyone here. I'll make a few calls and see what we can come up with. We'll figure this out."

Annie gave her a grateful look. "Thanks, Hannah. I don't know what I'd do without you."

"Right back at you, sis. It's so good having you back home again."

"It's good to be home," Annie said. "Until I came back here, I didn't realize how much I'd missed you and Dad."

"And Noah?" Hannah prompted.

"And Noah, yes." Annie's face relaxed into a tender calm as she glanced at the glittering engagement ring on her finger. The small diamond was modest, but classic, a perfect complement to Annie's unfussy, traditional style.

To Hannah, the best thing about the ring was the way it made her sister glow when she looked at it. "Are you two lovebirds talking about a date yet?"

Annie smiled and lifted her shoulder in a mild shrug. "A little. When Noah proposed a month ago, he said he didn't want to rush me into making any decisions before I was ready."

"So, are you? Ready, I mean."

Annie sank her teeth into her bottom lip as color rose into her cheeks. "I think so. It's been almost a year since Derek died in the motorcycle accident. I'll always miss him, but there was a part of my heart that had been reserved for Noah practically all my life. Now, that we have each other again, we're both eager to start making a new life together."

"I'm happy for you," Hannah said, reaching over to link their fingers the way they used to when they were kids. "You've come so far since you first returned home."

"You were a big part of that," Annie replied, her voice warm with affection. "You supported me and gave me comfort when I needed it the most. I can never thank you enough for being there for me, Hannah."

She squeezed Annie's hand. "I always will be. Just like you've been there for me."

Ever since they were little, they had always been close. After their mom died when Hannah was three years old, it had been Annie who'd looked out for Hannah and tried to provide the nurturing care and attention they'd both been missing.

Now that they were adults and both home in Crestpoint Beach, they were growing closer than ever. Hannah cherished her bond with Annie, and it buoyed her heart to see her older sister starting to thrive again after the tragedy she'd endured.

Annie stared at her now, tilting her head in question. "What about you, Hannah Banana?"

"What about me?"

Annie searched her eyes. "Are you happy?"

"Of course, I am." It wasn't a question Hannah spent a lot of time examining on her own, so her answer felt a little automatic. "I'll be even happier once we start checking off everything on that inspector's report."

Annie smiled in response, but she studied Hannah in a tender kind of silence, as if she could see right through the sunny outlook she strove to project.

On the surface, Hannah was happy. She could easily smile anyone's way and find things to be grateful about in her life, but there were times when her optimistic glow felt too much like a mask. There were pieces of her life that were missing, things that felt more and more out of her reach.

Seeing Annie so in love and excited about planning her future with Noah and his teenage daughter, Lainey, only made Hannah's longing for a family of her own more intense.

She had dated here and there, but love continued to elude her. And there were other dreams and yearnings she'd kept locked up inside her for so long, she wasn't even sure she'd know how to let them out.

She had countless blessings, to be sure. She had a family who loved her and a handful of good, true friends. She had a job that paid most of her bills, and while working at the gift shop wasn't a career like the one Annie had built for herself, Hannah genuinely enjoyed interacting with customers and meeting new people every day.

That simple job also gave her time to work on her true passion, art.

Maybe it was a stretch to call her crafty creations art, but she took great joy and satisfaction in the decorative things she made, from seashell wind chimes and jewelry, to her painted driftwood accents and small murals. Art had been her lifesaver, her refuge. It was the one thing she did purely for herself, for the fulfillment it brought her to take something ordinary or drab and turn it into a cheerful bit of whimsy.

Going into business with Annie on the beach house B&B was the first serious business undertaking Hannah had pursued, and she wasn't about to let a few small renovations and rickety stairs stand in the way of that goal.

Picking up the inspector's report, she rose from the sofa and gave Annie a determined look. "I'm going to start those phone calls now. Wish me luck."

Annie crossed her fingers on both hands. "Good luck!"

Grabbing her phone, Hannah walked out to the veranda to talk. She suspected it wouldn't be easy to find an available builder, but after half a dozen calls netted zero results, that suspicion was turning into a cold, hard reality.

She was just hanging up with yet another dead end when the screen door quietly creaked open behind her.

"Not going very well?" Annie asked cautiously.

Hannah sighed and slowly shook her head. "Everyone's booked solid. I even called a few places outside of town, but no one is available to do small renovations and repairs like ours while their crews are busy with bigger projects. Not even the local handyman has any extra time to help us out unless we can wait until after Memorial Day."

Annie folded her arms in front of her, a dejected look on her face. "So much for our plans to open in time for the big tourist season."

"I'm sorry, Annie."

"What for? It's not your fault."

"I'm the one who pushed you to do this," Hannah reminded her. "I know you were hoping the B&B revenue would help make up for the salary you turned down at the design firm in Jacksonville when you decided to stay in Crestpoint Beach."

Annie stepped over and curved her arm around Hannah's shoulders. "I'm right where I want to be. Here with you and Dad and Noah. If we can't open the house for guests until later than planned, that's okay. All I care about is that we're doing this together."

Hannah pivoted and drew her sister into her embrace. "That's all that matters to me, too."

As they hugged, a gentle breeze blew in off the turquoise waves. The salty air stirred the collection of seashell wind chimes Hannah had hung on the veranda, filling the quiet with the tinkling music of the shells.

The soft sound woke a memory in Hannah and she abruptly let go of her sister. "Annie! We have to call Henry Park."

"Noah's teacher friend?" Annie frowned in confusion. "Why? Does he moonlight as a handyman or something?"

"Not him," Hannah said, hardly able to contain her excitement. "But remember when we saw Henry at the school fundraiser you and Noah organized? He mentioned he had a friend who'd recently moved to town from Colorado. A friend who's a building contractor."

Annie's eyes lit up. "That's right. His name is Gabe. Henry bought one of your wind chimes as a housewarming gift for him."

Hannah nodded eagerly. "Do you think Henry's friend might be able to help us?"

"There's only one way to find out," Annie said. "Come on back inside. I'll call Noah and have him find out for us."

CHAPTER 2

*G*abe Lawson hauled an unopened cardboard box through his small rental cottage on the beach, his black T-shirt straining against the build of his upper arms and back. He set the box down in the kitchen with a huff before straightening back up, sweat beading on his brow.

Lifting his hand, he drew his fingers under the lower crown of his short, dark hair to sweep away the perspiration. "Is it always so hot here?"

His friend, Henry Park, chuckled as he walked into the kitchen with a smaller box under his arm. Henry had offered to lend a hand in emptying the small storage unit Gabe had rented for some of his belongings upon his arrival a month and a half ago.

"This is the cool season, buddy. Enjoy it while you can."

Gabe scoffed, shaking his head. It was hotter here in Florida at the beginning of March than it was back in Denver at the height of summer. If it wasn't for Henry's persuading him to move south for the year-round construction opportunities in Crestpoint Beach, Gabe would've chosen a cooler climate to spare himself the suffering.

"Give it time," Henry said. "You'll get used to it eventually."

Gabe slid him a dubious look, unsure he would be able to get over having endless sunshine and heat all during the year. He had moved to an entirely different environment than the one where he'd grown up in Colorado. It was a stark change of scenery here, but even he had to admit being on the beach in the tiny cottage he'd officially moved into earlier in the week was nice and different.

Different was what he'd needed the most after the way things had gone in Denver. He'd wanted a clean state, a chance to start fresh.

Gabe hoped he'd have that opportunity here in the quaint beach town where his best friend had relocated for his job teaching math at the local high school.

"I don't think it's possible to get used to living on the surface of the sun," he quipped, reaching for his glass of water. He downed it in a few long gulps, still feeling as if he were standing inside an oven, even within the shelter of the cottage.

Thankfully, there was a small breeze filtering through the open windows today. It brought with it the fresh scent of the ocean and the musical sounds of the painted seashell wind chime that danced in the soft gusts coming off the beach. It was the sole decoration he'd put up so far, and something about the quirky housewarming gift from Henry always managed to put a smile on Gabe's face.

"You know, you might be more comfortable if you invested in some tank tops," Henry pointed out. "Maybe something with a little color. You stand out like a sore thumb in all those drab clothes you brought with you from Colorado."

"I like drab," Gabe deadpanned. "I'll leave the surfer dude colors and wild patterns to you, my friend."

Henry smirked as he opened one of the many cardboard boxes littered throughout the open space of the cottage. Most of the rooms were fairly empty, other than the meager furnishings that had come with the one-bedroom rental.

The kitchen appliances were small and aged, but functional, and the living area was equipped with a TV, a beige loveseat, and a couple of chairs that had seen better days. The rustic wood-plank floors were scuffed and a bit weathered like the rest of the place, but Gabe hadn't been looking for luxury. As a thirty-three-year-old single male who had moved to town solely to focus on restarting his career and reputation as a builder, he had everything he needed to get by in the small cottage.

The incredible beachfront location was just icing on the cake.

Some pretty great icing, in fact.

As for the town, Crestpoint Beach seemed like a true gem. Cute shops and family businesses lined the main streets. Friendly locals mingled with visiting tourists of all ages, everyone ready with a smile and wave, even for a stranger like him. The residential areas ranged from midcentury bungalows set a few blocks back from the ocean, to multimillion-dollar, palatial beachfront estates, grand old Victorians, cozy Craftsman-inspired homes, tiny cottages, and everything in between.

If he wanted to find an ideal place to set up shop again, he couldn't have found a better location. Now, all he needed were some contacts to begin establishing his client list.

He glanced at his friend as they moved more boxes into the kitchen. "I don't mean to sound ungrateful about everything you've done for me in this move, Henry. I'm sure I'll settle in here just fine."

Henry clapped his shoulder. "No worries. At least you've got an awesome place to hang out while you're getting your business off the ground. I've got to say, I'm a little jealous of this primo location."

Gabe laughed. "If it was any closer to the high school, I have a feeling you would've tried to scoop this cottage out from under me as soon as you heard it was up for rent."

"Never," Henry said, then he shrugged. "Okay, maybe I would have. Fortunately, I like you, so no hard feelings. Just promise me I can come visit with my surfboard now and then."

"You bet. Anytime."

"Sweet. I'll even give you a few lessons."

Gabe held up his hands. "Let's not get crazy. I like my feet firmly planted on the ground, thank you very much. That's never going to change."

They went back to their work, moving boxes off the porch and into the cottage. Leaving the only home Gabe had ever known hadn't been an easy decision, but it helped having a friend waiting on the other end of the long journey. Henry had been a good friend to him, a true friend. After what happened in Denver, Gabe understood the value of that friendship more than ever.

"So, the mountain man finally experiences the beach," Henry teased at him lightly as he nodded to one of the open windows facing the ocean. "Seriously, though, is it everything I promised it would be?"

"It's great," Gabe said, realizing what an understatement

that was as he stared out at the gem-colored, green-blue waves and their foamy white curls rolling gently toward the shore. As he watched, a trio of pelicans soared in formation over the water, while a few hundred feet out, a dolphin played in the surf.

"Now that you've had the keys for a few days, I hope you've taken some time to explore the beach."

"Not yet. I'll get to it."

"You'll get to it?" Henry gaped at him. "What are you waiting for?"

Gabe shrugged. He had mostly been spending his time in the cottage, trying to figure out his next steps. It shocked him that until a couple of months ago he'd been certain his life was completely laid out and on course for a solid, more-than-stable future.

He and his business partner, Wyatt, had built a thriving company together in Denver. Their business was booming, and Gabe had kept so busy in the field he could hardly find a break in between projects. Not that he ever complained about the work.

He loved the hustle and being able to create things with his hands. It was his passion and his gift, two things his father had passed down to him from the time Gabe was a boy tagging along to his dad's construction work sites every summer.

Wyatt preferred to work in the office, handling all of the crew scheduling and supply issues. Eventually, he took over the books. Gabe believed everything was moving on a smooth, upward trajectory until one day out of the blue, the payroll bounced. By then it was already too late to save the business. Wyatt confessed he had been embezzling from the company for months, using the stolen funds to pay for his gambling addiction.

Just like that, their business was over. Along with their friendship.

Now, Gabe was starting all over, his path unclear.

Glancing up from his unintended walk down memory lane, he found Henry still staring at him. "You're too serious, man. You need to loosen up a little. Hitting the beach to soak up some rays is the first thing I would've done when I got here. Then I would've fetched my board and rode a few of those waves. It's not too late for a little of both, if you're game?"

Gabe shook his head, chuckling. "I've got about a dozen boxes to unpack before I think about loafing around like I'm on vacation. Not everyone operates on impulse and instant gratification."

"You say that like it's a bad thing," Henry joked, picking up one of the last few boxes and carrying it into the bedroom.

Gabe picked up another and followed him, a smile tugging at his mouth. He was fully aware that Henry was the adrenaline junkie between the two of them, and always would be. He grew up in Denver as well, and they had known each other since elementary school.

Back then, Henry was constantly up to mischief or misadventure of some sort, while Gabe had to be the level-headed thinker of the pair to prevent them from getting into too much trouble together. There had been a part of him that envied his friend's fearlessness and freedom, but Gabe's strict father never would've tolerated such behavior from him.

"I'll grab the last box," Henry said, wiping his brow. "Then I think it's time for me to collect on that pizza and ice-cold beer you promised in exchange for this workout."

Gabe nodded. "That sounds like a plan."

As they headed back out to the living room, Henry's phone

rang in his back pocket. He took it out and glanced at the display. "It's my friend Noah calling. Give me a minute to take this, all right?"

"No problem," Gabe said. "I'll be outside."

He strode out to the small porch overlooking the beach. It really was beautiful, possibly as beautiful as the mountains. He watched the sunlight play over the water, intrigued by the way the clouds overhead shadowed the waves and turned them different shades of blue, green, and gray—similar to how the light could change the colors of the mountains and foothills back home in Colorado.

That wasn't home anymore. It was going to take some getting used to before he'd be able to say the word "home" and picture palm trees and sand instead of the steep, rugged peaks of the Rockies. Would he ever be able to consider Florida home?

He had made the conscious decision to start over somewhere new, not because he didn't love the place he'd been born and raised, but because he felt the need to find out if he could make a go of his life somewhere entirely different. Somewhere he could build his company back up from scratch, entirely on his own this time.

His own client list. His own reputation. His own sweat and toil.

He never wanted to wake up again and discover that everything he'd worked for had been gambled right out from under him by a business partner he thought he could trust.

This time, Gabe's success—or failure—would hinge solely on him.

As he stared out at the water, his thoughts turning, Henry's voice sounded behind him. "Yeah, I'm actually here with Gabe right now, so I'll ask him what he thinks about it as soon as we hang up. I think I can persuade him to do it."

Gabe gave Henry a curious look. He hadn't yet met Noah Davis, but Henry had talked up his teaching colleague and good friend quite a bit and he sounded like a good guy. Gabe wasn't sure how he'd factored into their conversation, but he was about to find out.

"Sounds good," Henry said. "Yep, I'll talk to you soon. Bye."

At his friend's wide grin, Gabe arched a brow. "Please don't tell me I'm about to get invited to go swimming with sharks or wrestling alligators with you and your buddy."

Henry laughed. "Interesting suggestions, but no. Noah's fiancée, Annie, and her sister, Hannah, are planning to turn their family beach house into a B&B. They've got a list of things that need to be updated or repaired before they can pass inspection and open for business."

"What kinds of things?"

"Noah mentioned the veranda and front steps, some bathroom adjustments, and a few other things. I'm sure the sisters can give you more info when you call to let them know you're available to take the job." Henry gave him a hopeful look. "You *are* available, right? Sounds like they really need the help."

"How soon are they looking for someone to start?"

"The sooner the better. They'd like to be open before Memorial Day, which means they'll need to pass another inspection and have everything in place well before then."

Gabe nodded as he considered. He was accustomed to bigger projects, but he had to admit he was itching to have anything to work on after being in town for over a month. He wasn't used to idle time. He much preferred to keep busy doing something productive.

The list of tasks Henry described sounded like it was more

suited to a handyman than a contractor with his years of experience. Still, he supposed it couldn't hurt to have a local business on his client list once he was ready to start hiring crews and taking on the larger projects he'd need in order to build his business.

"Okay, I'll do it. Text me the number, and I'll give them a call to go over the details."

"Great," Henry replied, tapping the number into a message that hit Gabe's phone a moment later. "According to Noah, they're really in a tough spot, so thanks for helping out."

"I'll get them where they need to be," Gabe promised.

"I have no doubts," Henry said. "The Taylor sisters don't realize it yet, but they've just landed the best builder in Crestpoint Beach."

"Thanks for the vote of confidence."

"Hey, what are friends for?" Henry grinned. "Now, what about that pizza and beer?"

"You just put me to work," Gabe reminded him. "First, I'm going to call my new clients and get the details about the job they need me to do. Then we can go fill our faces."

Gabe's mind was already churning on all of the things he'd need in order to get started on this new project. He'd already applied for his contractor's license and completed all of the paperwork the day after he arrived in town. He'd also taken the time to scope out the area's building supply stores, but he would still need to buy some tools to round out the collection he'd brought with him from Denver.

All in all, he was in good shape to begin as soon as he was needed at the beach house. He could hardly wait to see what he'd be working on.

Henry stared at him, then shook his head on a laugh. "I can

practically hear your brain working, Lawson. Do you even know how to relax?"

"I don't know what you mean."

"Exactly my point." Henry chuckled. "Come on, I'll drive. You can make your call to the Taylors on the way to Slice of Paradise."

As he followed his friend out to his car, Gabe reflected on the fact that Henry was right about his inability to let loose. Sure, he worked too much and likely always would, but he hadn't moved to a new town to slow down or allow himself to get lazy. He had come there with a single purpose, with something to prove to himself, if no one else.

Taking the project at the beach house was the first step in that plan.

As far as Gabe was concerned, nothing was more important than completing that job without a single delay or misstep.

His future in Crestpoint Beach depended on it.

CHAPTER 3

Hannah blew a loose spiral of her long blonde hair out of her face as she swept the sand off the beach house porch. She'd showed up early that next morning, hardly able to sleep ahead of her and Annie's first meeting with Gabe Lawson.

Although he had already accepted the job and quoted them a reasonable price sight-unseen over the phone, Hannah still wanted to make a good impression and that meant ensuring the house looked as appealing as possible. She didn't know if Gabe realized he was their only hope of opening the B&B on time, but she didn't want to give him any reason to back out of the project.

Not that she actually expected him to raise an eyebrow at some errant beach sand or a few cobwebs here and there. The truth was, she was nervous, and the way she burned off anxious energy was by keeping busy. With the porch swept clean, she zeroed in on the cluster of old spiderwebs hanging from the white lattice trim in the corner of the veranda and the house.

She still had a little time before Gabe was due to arrive. Once she finished spiffing up outside, she should have a few minutes to dash into the house to freshen up and trade her rainbow tie-dye tank top and pink shorts for the more presentable sundress she'd brought with her for the meeting.

Her hair could probably use some attention, too. The ponytail she'd gathered it into had turned into a frizzy mess in the humidity of the morning, with more escaped tendrils blowing into her face as the warm breeze shuttled in from the beach.

Hooking some of the strands behind her ear, she carried her long-handled broom to the other side of the veranda and reached up to dislodge the tattered webs. She wasn't as tall as her sister, so she had to grab the railing for balance as she strained to get the broom high enough. She grunted and huffed, jabbing at the high corner of the porch's ceiling.

"Ugh," she muttered under her breath. "Why did I have to get the short gene?"

She took another swipe at the cobwebs, hopping on her bare feet to reach the last of them. The weak porch railing creaked under her grasp as she put more pressure on the aged wood.

"Good morning."

Hannah froze at the unfamiliar male voice that sounded somewhere behind her. The low, measured baritone rolled through her senses, making her pulse skitter as she slowly brought the broom down and prepared to face the stranger.

Please, don't let it be Gabe, she silently prayed, wincing before she turned around.

The instant her eyes landed on the handsome man standing at the base of the veranda steps, the skitter in her pulse accelerated into a full-blown gallop. Tall and athletically fit, he had short hair the color of black coffee and pale green eyes that looked more inviting than the emerald water at his back. He wore a conservative light-blue button-down shirt with the sleeves rolled up over his muscled forearms. Slim-fit khakis accentuated his long legs, ending at the tops of his dark-brown boots.

Hannah hadn't known what to expect with regard to Henry's friend from Denver, but this strikingly good-looking man left her thoughts in a scatter.

He stared at her in mild curiosity while she struggled to form a coherent greeting. "Are you Annie?"

She shook her head. "Um. Hannah."

His squared jaw lifted in acknowledgment. "I'm Gabe Lawson."

"You're early," she murmured, trying not to think about how sweaty and…colorful she must look in her cleaning attire.

He glanced at his watch. "Actually, I'm right on time. Nine o'clock on the dot."

"Oh," Hannah said, offering a smile and hoping she didn't appear as flustered as she felt. So much for wanting to look presentable. She leaned the broom against the house and gestured to him. "Well, come on in. My sister, Annie, is waiting inside."

"Great." He walked up the short steps, his gaze sweeping over the veranda as if he were already taking a mental account of the work ahead of him. His eyes paused on her collection of painted-seashell wind chimes that swayed and jingled in the breeze. "I've got one just like these at my place. My friend Henry gave it to me."

"I know," she replied. "I made it."

"No kidding?" His firm mouth curved in the first glimmer

of a smile. It was there and gone in a blink, however, replaced by the all-business expression that had greeted her upon his arrival. "Sounds like you and your sister have a bit of work for me to do around here. Shall we get started?"

"Sure." His abrupt shift from friendly to focused took her aback a little, but she brushed it off as she opened the screen door and led him inside the house. "Annie," she called into the quiet house. "Gabe Lawson is here."

"So soon?" Annie's voice carried down from the third floor. "Isn't he early?"

"Nope, he's right on time. Nine o'clock on the dot."

Hannah slanted him a wry glance as she repeated what he'd told her a few moments ago. For all the good it did. Her attempt at humor seemed lost on him. He stood as stiffly as a soldier beside her, except for his gaze, which continued its silent assessment of his surroundings while they waited in an awkward silence for Annie to join them.

She glided down the stairs in white Bermuda shorts, a sleeveless floral blouse, and sandals. Her sleek shoulder-length blonde hair looked flawless, as always.

"Hi, Gabe. Thanks for coming to our rescue, especially on such short notice."

He shook Annie's offered hand. "Happy to help."

While they greeted each other, Hannah stared down at her bare toes and the ten different colors of nail polish she'd painted on them a couple of nights ago. She and Annie were night-and-day in terms of style and personality. That fact had never bothered Hannah before, but standing next to Gabe while her older sister introduced herself to him made Hannah wish she possessed a little of Annie's easy style and effortless poise.

Gabe pulled a folded sheet of paper out of the back pocket

of his khakis. "I brought a printout of the inspector's report you emailed me. As I said on the phone, I don't anticipate any issues in completing everything ahead of your timeline."

Annie smiled. "That's such a relief to hear. Right, Hannah?"

"Yeah," she agreed cheerfully. "You're a real lifesaver, Gabe."

He spared her only a fleeting glance before unfolding the report. "I'm prepared to get started this morning on some of the items, but we should go over a few of them just so we're all on the same page."

"Of course," Annie replied.

As he began reviewing the inspector's list with them, Hannah couldn't help but notice that he seemed inclined to dive right into business, as if he didn't have the time—or the interest—for small talk. He wasn't unfriendly exactly, but he definitely wasn't warm and inviting either. Maybe that was simply the difference between folks who lived in a small town like Crestpoint Beach versus people from a big city like Denver.

Hannah was used to making fast friends of everyone she met, including the total strangers who passed through the Gift Emporium when she was on shift. She prided herself on her ability to draw a smile out of even the most reticent grump or cranky kid, but so far Gabe Lawson presented a challenge she'd rarely encountered.

Part of her appreciated his almost singular focus on getting right to the point of why he was there, but she wouldn't have minded if he slowed down a bit and allowed a minute for them to get familiar with one another. After all, he was going to be working at the house on a fairly regular basis until the work was finished, so it would be nice to know something about him.

Besides all that, Hannah was just plain curious about him as well.

"Henry mentioned you recently moved here from Colorado," she said, seizing on a pause in his explanation of sprinkler system options to interject some light conversation. "After living near mountains, how are you enjoying all of this flat land in Florida?"

"It's different," he replied with a shrug. "I'm sure I'll adjust in time."

"So, does that mean you've relocated here permanently?"

"I'm not sure yet." He glanced at her, a small crease forming between the dark slashes of his brows. "It'll depend on how my business does here, I suppose."

Hannah offered him a reassuring smile. "I'm sure it'll do great. There's always a lot of new construction and renovations going on here in town."

"Good to know," he said, then turned his attention back to the inspector's notes. "When we spoke on the phone, Annie, you mentioned wanting to make one of the first-floor bedrooms and the bathroom wheelchair accessible, but I don't see that flagged on this inspection report."

"That's right," Annie said. "Hannah and I had already agreed we wanted to make those alterations before we open for business, even though we're not required by law to do it."

"Nice," he replied, his green eyes moving briefly from Annie to Hannah. A flicker of warmth glowed in his gaze for the instant their eyes met. "I can take care of that for you, no problem."

Hannah felt her cheeks warm from just that momentary crack in his hard shell. "How long have you been in construction, Gabe?"

"Pretty much my whole life," he replied without looking up from the report. He paused then, as if he didn't really want to say more. "My dad used to be a builder, so I learned the trade from watching him and going with him to job sites when I was a kid."

Hannah smiled, wondering what Gabe must have looked like as a cute little boy trailing after his father. Was he always this serious and tight-lipped even then? What did Gabe do for fun when he was a kid?

"So, did you and your dad work together before you came here?"

"No." He lifted his gaze as if surprised she was still quizzing him. "My father's been retired for a long time."

"Our dad's retired, too," she said. "He used to operate the lighthouse here in town, but now it's managed by the National Park Service. It's a really pretty light, just a short walk down the beach from here. You should make time to go see it sometime."

He grunted noncommittally. "Thanks for the tip."

She was getting the sense that he expected his short replies to discourage her from asking more questions. He clearly didn't know her, because she loved a challenge. It didn't hurt that Gabe Lawson was incredibly attractive. He smelled good, too. More than once, she caught herself leaning a fraction closer to him if only to breathe in more of his clean, woodsy scent.

"Did you work for a big construction company in Colorado?"

He seemed to stiffen at the inquiry. It took him longer to answer this question than any of the others she'd fired off, and when he finally did, it was a brisk reply. "I owned a business with a partner for the past nine years."

"Nine years? That's quite a while. What made you decide to move here?"

His gaze flattened as he glanced at her, and it was almost as if a door had just slammed shut in front of her. "The partnership didn't work out."

She drew back. "Oh. I'm sorry."

He didn't respond, and she felt awkward for wading into an obviously touchy subject.

Here she'd thought she was making a little progress with getting him to loosen up, but now he seemed more determined than ever to avoid eye contact with her, never mind continuing their conversation.

Annie glanced between them as a prolonged silence settled. "Would you like a quick tour of the house, Gabe?"

"Sure, that would be great. Annie, you mentioned you're living here at the house full-time?"

"Yes, on the third floor, but I'll be staying with my fiancé while you're working here."

Gabe nodded. "What about you, Hannah? Do you live here, too?"

It was the first time he'd actually used her name, and the sound of it on his lips sent an uninvited heat into her cheeks. "No, I live at home with our father."

"She's been taking care of Dad for several years," Annie interjected. "His arthritis has really been slowing him down, so Hannah moved back in to look after him."

Gabe's eyes lingered on Hannah while Annie spoke. He cleared his throat. "Well, it's a good thing neither of you will be trying to get any sleep here when I'm on site. I'll be doing a lot of hammering and sawing. I'm also going to be creating a lot of dust, but don't worry about your furniture. I'll bring plenty of covers for everything, and I'll put paper down on the floor so I don't scuff anything up."

Hannah smiled at him. "Thanks. That's really considerate of you."

"Just part of the job." He refolded the inspector's report and slid it back into his pocket. "If you don't mind, before you show me around the place I'm going to head out to my truck and grab my tools and a few supplies. Since I'm here, I might as well get started on some measurements and tackle a few of the smaller items on the list."

They both nodded at him, and he turned around and strode out of the house. The screen door groaned behind him as it swung shut, then his boots thumped in retreat off the porch.

When he was out of sight and earshot, Hannah slid a look at her sister. "Do you think he'll come back, or did I annoy him to death with all of my chatter and questions?"

Annie laughed quietly and shook her head. "You were just trying to be friendly. There's no harm in that."

"Tell it to Gabe." Hannah let go of a sigh. She didn't want to be negative, but she couldn't keep her reservations to herself. "Do you really think this is a good idea, Annie?"

"You mean, opening the B&B?"

"No, I mean him. Gabe. He's not very personable. Did you notice how every time I tried to say something to him, he grumbled a few words and went right back to business?"

Annie shrugged. "Maybe he's just a serious person."

Hannah couldn't argue that. Gabe Lawson seemed to take "serious" to the extreme. She frowned. "Would it kill him if he smiled once in a while? He acted as if I was interrogating him and I was only trying to break the ice. I mean, we don't really know anything about this man, and he's going to be in our house every day for the next few weeks, tearing it apart."

Annie laughed softly. "He's fixing up the place, not tearing it down." She tilted her head quizzically. "I think the real problem you might be having with Gabe is that you're attracted to him."

Even though it was true, Hannah scoffed. "What's attractive about a cold brick wall?"

Annie pursed her lips. "Mm, hm. Well, attractive or not, we didn't hire him for his conversation skills. Fortunately for us, Gabe's got two more important things we do need—experience and availability. Don't forget, he also quoted us a great price since we're his first project in Crestpoint Beach."

All valid points and Hannah had no time to debate a single one of them, anyway. The jangle of Gabe's toolbox announced his return as he rounded the front of the house and stepped back onto the veranda. He wiped his boots on the welcome mat, knocking lightly on the screen door before opening it.

"I have a basic agreement for us to sign," he said, holding up a manila folder in his free hand. "It's nothing too complicated, just something to protect both parties and lay out our mutual expectations so there are no surprises."

"Oh, that's great," Annie replied. "I'll go find a pen so we can sign it."

Although Hannah was certain she'd seen at least half a dozen pens in one of the kitchen drawers, Annie darted upstairs instead, leaving Hannah standing alone with Gabe in the living area. After their awkward start when he arrived, Hannah found herself at an uncustomary loss for words with him now.

To her shock, Gabe filled the silence.

"This is a beautiful house. Nothing beats the charm of a grand old Victorian."

"I totally agree," she replied, offering a tentative smile. "My grandparents built this house back in the Thirties. They lived here until they both passed, and for a while Annie and I lived here with our parents while Grandpa Joe and Grandma Betsy were still alive."

Gabe nodded in response. While he was far from a sparkling conversationalist, Hannah was willing to count this momentary glimpse of a less rigid side of him as a win.

"There was a lot of love in this house over the years," she said, attempting to pull him a bit farther out of his shell. "Annie and I are hoping our guests at the B&B will feel some of that love when they stay here, too."

He gave her another polite nod. "Well, I'll do my best to get things where they need to be so you can make that possible. Seems like you've got the interior design side well under control. Whoever did all of the updates and decorating in here has done a great job preserving the character of the place."

"That's all Annie's doing," Hannah admitted. "My only design contributions were the wind chimes out on the veranda and some seashell lamps in a few of the guest rooms."

Gabe smiled as if he thought she was just being modest, but the sad fact was, it was true.

Hannah felt woefully inadequate when she compared her own efforts to Annie's in reviving the old house and creating a comfortable nest for their future guests to enjoy. Her sister never made her feel that she wasn't an integral part of their shared project, but deep down Hannah wished there was something she could point to with pride inside the house and know that she did it all on her own.

"Found one!" Annie called out as she came back downstairs with a pen in her hand. She gave Hannah a knowing grin. "Okay, Gabe, show us where to sign and let's make this official."

"Sure."

He set down his toolbox and carried the manila folder over to the dining room table in the open concept living area. Patiently, he went over all of the terms of the agreement with them.

Annie's point about grading Gabe on his abilities rather than his personality was a sound one, and some of Hannah's earlier misgivings about him eased as she listened to his thoughtful explanations about the work he would be doing and his confident demeanor as he reviewed his plans for deliverables and completion.

By the time they had finished and each signed the document in duplicate, Hannah was left without any doubt that the beach house was in good, capable hands. Even if the one doing the holding still seemed as if he'd rather be anywhere than in the same room with her.

"That's all I need to get started," Gabe said, folding up his copy of the agreement and leaving them with the one inside the folder.

He reached out and shook Annie's hand, then turned to Hannah to do the same.

His fingers closed around hers, his grasp warm and strong. It was nothing but a professional gesture, yet every nerve ending in her body lit up like a Christmas tree. She made the mistake of meeting his gaze and as those intense green eyes stared back at her she felt a surge of heat flood into her cheeks.

He dropped her hand as if it had burned him and cleared his throat. "How about that house tour now?"

CHAPTER 4

That evening around sunset, Gabe was just taking some leftover pizza out of the ancient little microwave in his cottage when someone knocked on the front door.

"Yeah. Be right there."

Dropping the soggy paper plate with its slice of reheated sausage-and-pepperoni onto the counter, he crossed the short distance from the kitchenette and opened the door. Henry Park stood on the other side of the screen next to another man Gabe guessed to be around their same age.

"Hey, Henry." Gabe glanced from his friend to the taller man beside him as he invited the pair inside. "What's going on?"

Henry grinned. "Gabe, this is Noah Davis. Noah, this is Gabe Lawson. Noah teaches Biology at the high school."

Gabe gave the man with brown hair and hazel eyes a nod of greeting. "Annie's fiancé, right? Nice to meet you, Noah."

"Likewise, Gabe." Noah shook his hand. "Annie tells me

you've officially started working at the beach house as of this morning."

"That's right. Beautiful place. I've got a feeling it's going to be a very successful B&B."

"Yes, I think so, too. Annie and Hannah have poured a lot of effort and emotion into preparing it to open."

"I noticed. I'm looking forward to getting started on the updates and fixes." Gabe slid a curious look at Henry. "I don't imagine you guys came all the way out here tonight just to say hi."

Knowing his friend, there was some ulterior motive for the fact that he hadn't called before showing up with Noah. Henry was on some kind of mission and Gabe had a feeling he was at the center of it.

Noah cleared his throat. "Sorry for showing up unannounced. Henry said it was the only way."

"The only way for what?"

"To get you out of the house to toast the landing of your first project in Crestpoint Beach," Henry blurted around a chuckle. "You probably haven't paused to have anything for dinner yet."

"Actually, I was just about to have some pizza from the other day while I went over a few things ahead of my workday tomorrow."

Henry crossed his arms over his chest. "Not tonight, Lawson. Pitch the leftovers, ditch the work for a couple of hours, and come with us. We're taking you to Coco's Beachside Bar and we're not taking no for an answer."

Even if Gabe was tempted to beg off, he knew how stubborn Henry could be when he really wanted something. Gabe had already been to Coco's a couple of times, and he had to admit the thought of a burger with their signature crab dip and chips with a view of the ocean sounded a lot more appealing than another night holed up in his cottage with a plate of rubbery, two-day-old pizza.

He cuffed Henry on the shoulder. "Actually, it sounds great. Thanks, you guys."

"Awesome," Henry said. "Let's go. It's close enough up the beach to walk there."

Gabe dumped his pizza in the trash, then stepped into the pair of flip-flops he'd purchased in town with Henry a couple afternoons ago. Slipping his wallet and keys into the front pocket of his shorts, he followed his two companions out to the balmy sunset waiting outside.

Coco's Beachside Bar was about a half-mile up the shore from Gabe's cottage. Hut-like in appearance, with a faux thatched roof and live music playing on the outdoor patio that sat just off the sand, the place was always packed with locals and tourists who seemed to enjoy the laidback, tropical vibe as much as the delicious food and drinks Coco's served up day and night.

Instead of going inside to the air-conditioned seating area, Henry and Noah led Gabe along the short boardwalk at the back of the restaurant. Tonight, a Reggae band played island classics for the diners seated at the dozens of tables situated on the patio. The glow from the brick fire pit in the center of the area cast an orange hue on everything, contrasting with the gathering night that would soon shroud the nearby beach in darkness.

Seating at Coco's was first-come, first-served, so when a four-top opened up just as Gabe and his friends arrived, they moved in to claim it. A waitress greeted them with menus and a recited list of specials from both the kitchen and the bar. After placing their order for appetizers and draft beers, they settled in to enjoy the music and the warm breeze rolling off the Gulf.

"You really got lucky scoring that cottage, Gabe," Noah said. "People can wait a year or more to find an affordable rental right on the beach."

Gabe nodded, pausing to answer while their server delivered their drinks and a big basket of warm, homemade chips and bowl of Coco's famous crab dip. The three of them dug in as soon as the food hit the table.

"The cottage may be small, but there's no beating that awesome location," Henry said around a mouthful of crunchy chips. "I told Gabe he's going to owe me one massive favor in return someday for getting him in there."

Gabe smiled at his friend. "Name it, anytime. The cottage sure beats the noisy duplex I was renting month-to-month outside of town when I first got here."

Henry saluted him with his glass. "Stick with me, Lawson. I've got your back."

Gabe raised his in return. "And I've got yours, buddy. Just like old times."

It felt good hanging out with someone he knew he could trust and always had. Noah seemed like a good guy, too. He had a calm demeanor and an inquisitiveness in his steady gaze that seemed to suit him as a teacher.

He looked at Gabe as he took a drink, then set his glass down on the table. "How are you settling in so far?"

"Not bad. I'm feeling a lot better now that I've got a job to work on again. I'm not used to being in between projects."

"Gabe doesn't know what idle time is," Henry added with a smirk. "I actually think he's allergic to vacations."

Gabe grunted at the good-natured jab. "All of that may be true, but I also happen to love my work."

"Nothing wrong with that," Noah said, dragging a chip through the thick dip before popping it into his mouth.

Gabe took another chip, too, savoring the creamy goodness of the food and the comfortable camaraderie around the table. He'd had many colleagues and acquaintances in Denver, but his long hours on the job and his lack of interests outside work had kept him at a distance from most people.

Once the business with Wyatt had gotten successful, it became harder and harder to tell who was inviting him along to things because they truly wanted his company or because they thought they had something to gain from it.

Consequently, for many years, his closest friendship had been with Wyatt. Or so he'd believed. After the way he'd been so blindsided by Wyatt's betrayal, Gabe wasn't eager to let anyone get close to him ever again.

The one thing he knew he could rely on was his commitment to his work.

Still, he had to admit he was having a pretty good time tonight. Henry was like a brother to him despite the distance that had separated them until now, and Noah made it easy to relax and let down his guard a little.

If he thought about it, everyone he'd met in Crestpoint Beach so far had been genuinely warm and welcoming.

In particular, Hannah Taylor.

She hadn't been far from his mind since he'd met her that morning. He could still picture her leaning on the railing of the veranda in her tank top and shorts, muttering to herself and hopping on her bare feet as she attempted to dislodge a stubborn spiderweb.

With her wavy, long blonde hair and rainbow-hued clothing, she'd been a startling burst of color and vivaciousness that had taken him totally by surprise as he'd arrived at the beach house.

Then she'd turned around to face him and he nearly swallowed his tongue at how stunningly beautiful she was.

Both sisters were gorgeous, but it was quirky, sunny Hannah who totally captivated him. Where Annie was elegant and poised, Hannah burned with so much energy and warmth she lit up the entire room. It had taken all of Gabe's concentration to keep his thoughts centered on the job at hand whenever she smiled at him or gazed at him with her big blue eyes. Even her sweet, slightly breathless voice did something funny to his pulse, so he'd done his best to keep their conversations to a minimum and focused solely on the house.

He shook his head, reflecting that she probably thought he was a bore, or worse, an unfriendly jerk. He wasn't used to sharing things about his personal life, and Hannah was the kind of person who seemed to hold nothing back.

Just one more reason why he would do best to block out any distractions that kept him from focusing on his work. What mattered to him most was completing the beach house updates ahead of schedule and ensuring that his first project in town was a success.

Failure on any level was simply not an option he would accept.

His new business in Crestpoint Beach needed a solid foundation, and that meant keeping his eye on that goal, not on pretty Hannah Taylor.

He cleared his throat, realizing he'd gone adrift in his thoughts for a few minutes while Henry and Noah chatted about things going on at the school.

"How long have you been teaching, Noah?"

"I received my teaching degree about four years after my

daughter was born, so it's going on twelve years now."

"Wow, long time," Gabe replied. "So, you have a teenager?"

"Yeah. Her name's Lainey." His face filled with fatherly pride and affection. "She's an amazing kid, if I do say so myself."

Henry nodded in agreement, smiling. "She's basically the sixteen-year-old female version of you, Noah. It's crazy how similar you two are."

"True, but don't let her mother hear you say that." Chuckling warmly, Noah glanced at Gabe. "My ex, Claudia, and I divorced about five years ago."

"Sorry," Gabe said. "Divorce is tough, especially on the kids."

"I know. My folks split up when I was thirteen," Noah divulged. "Sounds like you speak from experience, too?"

Gabe nodded. "I was fourteen when mine broke up. My sister, Sabrina, and I lived with my mom after the divorce. My parents never got along particularly well, but after they separated it was like a war zone between them."

Noah frowned, sympathy in his hazel eyes. "That sounds rough. I'm sorry you went through that. My father simply woke up one morning and left. Probably for the best. I've told myself all my life that if I could do just one thing right, I'd be a better father to my kids than he was."

"And you are," Henry reassured him. "Lainey's proof enough of that."

Noah took a sip of his beer. "I'm just glad Claudia's loosening up on the reins with her a bit more now. I've got Annie to thank for that. I never would've imagined that my ex-wife and my fiancée would be getting along so well. Annie's the glue holding all of us together."

After meeting Annie, Gabe wasn't surprised to learn of her

kindness and understanding, even when it came to the woman Noah had once been married to. There had been a gentleness to her that even Gabe had noticed in the short time he'd spent at the house.

"Annie seems like a special woman," he told his new friend. "Congrats on your engagement, by the way."

He smiled. "Thanks. Annie is amazing. So is Hannah, in fact."

Henry wiggled his brows at Gabe. "And Hannah's single, too. You know, in case you were wondering."

Gabe nearly choked on his beer. "Thank you for that unsolicited personal detail about one of my clients."

Henry chuckled. "Don't tell me you didn't notice that Hannah's a knockout."

"I noticed," he muttered under his breath. "Did you miss the part where I said she's a client? I don't mix business with pleasure."

Henry held up his hands. "Hey, I'm just trying to help be your wingman."

"More like wingnut," Gabe shot back with wry humor. "If you want to help me with anything, stick to restaurant recommendations. This place is my becoming my new favorite."

Henry looked at Noah across the table from him. "I think he's trying to change the subject."

"Kind of seems like it to me, too," Noah agreed, amusement tugging at his lips.

Gabe smirked, staring down into his glass and shaking his head.

"At least I now know there are two guys I need to avoid if I ever need advice on women, which I won't," he said, playing along despite the rapid beating of his heart when it came to Hannah.

For all his nonchalance, Gabe couldn't help but feel that a part of him was missing on the inside. There was a space in his soul that felt empty, something he tended to avoid acknowledging, even to himself. No matter how challenging and rewarding his work life was, no project had ever been able to fill that void, to make him feel completely whole.

He had a deep longing inside him—a loneliness—and he couldn't help but wonder if that part of him would feel empty forever.

Mentally shaking himself out of his sulk, he shot a wry glance at Henry. "Maybe you're the one who needs help in the dating arena. After all, I don't see you rushing out to find the love of your life."

"Already met her," Henry replied, tilting his beer to his lips. "Her name's adrenaline and we are very happy together."

Gabe and Noah laughed, both raising their glasses to meet Henry's toast to his own joke. After they all drank, Henry leaned over to knock his shoulder against Gabe's.

"You know I'm just messing with you about Hannah, right? She's too fun for you, anyway. No offense, buddy."

"None taken. I'm sure you're right about that."

From his brief encounter with her that morning, it was obvious they were about as opposite as they could be.

She was bubbly and outgoing. He was serious and guarded.

She seemed like the kind of woman who made everything fun, while the only thing he knew how to do was work.

Not that any of those contrasts mattered, because he'd meant it when he said he never mixed business with pleasure.

As long as he was working on the beach house, Hannah Taylor was off-limits in every way.

CHAPTER 5

With a wince, Hannah ducked away from a plume of hot steam that rose from the pan of chicken she was searing for her father's dinner.

When he was first diagnosed with rheumatoid arthritis, it worried her, especially when seeing him painfully shuffle around the house or struggle to curl his fingers around something he used to handle with ease. She and Annie had already lost their mom when they were kids. Hannah couldn't bear the thought of watching her dad's health slowly decline, too.

Although there were times she wished she was living in her own place instead of sharing the bungalow where she'd spent the better part of her childhood, it was easier to keep an eye on her dad and be around if he needed help with anything. Besides, it wasn't as if she had a thriving social life to worry about.

Sure, she had her many friends in town. Between the guys she went to school with and the revolving door of single male newcomers who came to Crestpoint Beach for vacations or fresh starts, she had plenty of opportunities to date, too. But the truth was, as open and friendly as she was in her day-to-day life, she had little interest in casual or temporary relationships.

Deep down, she yearned for the unbreakable connection she saw in Annie and Noah, or in the forever kind of love both her parents and grandparents had shared. At the age of thirty, she wondered if she would ever be able to find any man who could live up to the dream she held so close in her heart.

Nor could she fathom why pondering happily-ever-afters would send her thoughts swirling back to Gabe Lawson.

If she were being honest with herself, her thoughts had been hovering around him all day, which only added to her frustration with the man.

As handsome as he was, the gruff, all-business contractor couldn't be more different from her ideal man if he'd tried. At least he'd seemed to make a small attempt at conversation before she and Annie had given him the tour of the beach house, but he'd still acted as if he couldn't get away from her fast enough.

With a frown knitting her forehead, Hannah pushed the pieces of lean chicken breast around in the pan, then opened the oven door to check on the roasted vegetables she'd made. Her father wouldn't be excited about the heart-healthy mix of broccoli, carrots, and cauliflower, but she and Annie were in agreement that his diet could use some adjustments.

Hannah typically ate dinner with him when she wasn't at work, but she'd had a quick sandwich with Annie at the beach house before she'd left to come home to the bungalow a few streets away. As she stirred the vegetables and set the timer for another ten minutes, she heard her father entering the house from the front door.

"It sure smells good in here," Frank Taylor said, his footsteps shuffling slowly as he made his way into the kitchen.

Three times a week, he and a pair of widowed buddies met at another old friend's house just down the street to play cards. Hannah wasn't sure who started the tradition, but she knew it did her father a great deal of good to have the company and the conversation every week. She smiled to herself as he entered the kitchen behind her.

"I hope you didn't spoil your appetite with a lot of chips and pretzels again, Dad."

"No ma'am," he said with a chuckle. His hand came to rest on her shoulder while he peeked into the pan. "Is that the garlic chicken breast I like?"

"Sure is. I made you a nice veggie medley to go with it, too."

He made a less enthusiastic noise in the back of his throat. "Let me guess. Broccoli?"

She laughed softly as she glanced at him. "You can't live on mashed potatoes and gravy or mac'n'cheese, Dad."

"Says who?" he grumbled, leaning in to kiss her cheek. "You know, you and your sister really don't need to make such a fuss over me, honey. I'm sure you have better things to do than spend your evenings fixing dinner for me."

It wasn't the first time he'd said it, and even though he was far from helpless, Hannah saw no point in allowing him to struggle in the kitchen. She'd learned a long time ago that he acted the toughest when he was feeling his worst. Being a proud man who'd devoted his life to supporting his two daughters on his own after their mother, Ginny, died, Frank Taylor would never ask anyone for help, no matter how badly he needed it. That went double when it came to imposing on Hannah or Annie.

"I don't mind a bit, Dad. Besides, you know Annie and I enjoy bossing you around for a change."

He chuckled. "Well, I'll buy that, I suppose."

"Did you have fun with the guys tonight?"

"Oh, yeah. Tonight was Euchre night. Vince and I dominated the table. Poor Chuck and Ruben didn't know what hit them." He grinned and wiggled his brows. "Too bad we only play for points, or they'd really be upset with us."

Hannah smiled, grateful that her father still kept up his old friendships and that he felt well enough to get out and socialize now and then. Aside from his physical limitations, he was too young at heart to spend his time alone. Secretly, Hannah hoped that someday he might find a lady friend to spend time with, or maybe even fall in love again.

"Speaking of getting out and having fun," he hedged. "Shouldn't you be doing the same thing, sweetheart?"

"I have plenty of fun staying in with you, Dad. If I wanted to hang out with my friends, I would."

"Okay, honey. If you say so." He sighed, giving her shoulder a gentle pat. "I'm going to go wash up and get ready to eat. Aren't you joining me?"

She shrugged. "Annie and I had a bite before I came home, so I'm fine."

"You mean I have to enjoy all of those *healthy* vegetables by myself?"

He winked as he said it and she gave him a wry look. "Oh, maybe I'll have a small plate of them with you."

"Wonderful," he said. "You can tell me all about your meeting with that contractor fella you girls hired to get the old house ready for business."

Hannah barely stifled her groan at the reminder of Gabe

Lawson. "All right. I'll put dinner on the table while you're cleaning up."

Her father shuffled down the hallway, and she filled a plate for him with the herbed chicken and a decent helping of the roasted vegetables. She put a spoonful on a small plate for herself, then set everything out on the table for them.

They spent a pleasant hour chatting together while they ate, and her dad was apparently so engrossed in the conversation that he left not even as much as a crumb on his plate by the time they finished chatting. Affection shone in his blue eyes as he regarded her across the small dining table, a tender smile playing at the edge of his mouth.

"What's that look about, Dad?"

"You, sweetheart." He reached out and covered her hand with his. "It's nice to see you and your sister working together on the beach house, making plans to fill it with life again. I'm really proud of you girls and all the love you've poured into Grandpa Joe and Grandma Betsy's home. I know they'd be proud, too. And your mom."

Hannah smiled, her vision turning a bit watery as emotion pricked the back of her eyes. "Thanks, Dad. It means a lot to hear you say that."

She also couldn't help feeling that some of the credit he gave her was misplaced. Turning the house into a bed-and-breakfast had been her idea initially, but it was Annie who championed the project. It was Annie who understood just how to blend the historic beauty of the Victorian home with the comforts of the present. Her design fingerprints were on every piece of furniture and fabric choice.

She had given Hannah the liberty to weigh in with her own recommendations and ideas throughout the transformation, but there was no denying that the house would only be a shadow of its current spectacular state without Annie's vision. Hannah felt that truth today, when she and her sister had given Gabe a tour of every room and living area.

Her father was right that she and Annie had poured a lot of love into the place, but what Hannah hadn't yet been able to give it was a piece of herself.

"Dinner was delicious, honey," her father announced after a few moments. "Now, I think I'll help you clean up the dishes, then have a little nap in front of the TV."

Standing slowly, he picked up his plate and reached for hers.

Hannah smiled as she got up from her chair. "I've got this, Dad. You go relax."

"I need to earn my keep around here."

She gave him a pointed look, resting her fisted hands on her hips. "It'll go twice as fast if I do it by myself, so out of my kitchen."

"Since when did I raise such bossy daughters?" He chuckled as he carried the plates to the sink. On his way past her, he paused to buss her cheek. "Thank you for taking such good care of me, sweetheart. I love you."

"Love you, too, Dad."

She washed the dishes and cleaned everything up while he settled into his favorite recliner in the living room, the laugh track from a sitcom filtering through the small house.

Hannah turned off the kitchen light when she was finished, then walked down the hallway to her childhood bedroom where she'd slept since moving back in with him. Inside the room was a twin bed and painted dresser, surrounded by a somewhat organized chaos of art supplies and crafting materials.

Paints in dozens of colors, broken and intact shells of all

shapes and sizes, sketchbooks, pencils, and string were scattered all over her room, covering the carpeted floor, her desk, the top of her dresser, her bed, and her windowsill.

As cluttered as it was, being surrounded by so much color and the tools she used to make her art never failed to lift her spirits. She felt most alive when she was creating things, whether it was a simple embellished seashell or a painting she brought into being on a piece of driftwood or a canvas. There was something so captivating about brush strokes creating something beautiful right in front of her eyes. Being able to share her art with others was even more gratifying because it gave her the ability to see how her creations brought pleasure or inspiration to someone else.

It was only a hobby, but there was a part of her that wished it could be more someday.

With a sigh, she let her gaze drift to the wall behind her bed, she had painted a large mural of the beach back when she was in high school. At the time, her creativity had soared as high and as limitless as her dreams. She had painted on everything she could find, endlessly inspired and fearless in her expression.

She didn't know where that young artist had gone, but she missed her.

Some days, she wasn't even sure she'd recognize her anymore.

Hannah stared at the whimsical ocean mural with its white-capped waves of deep blues and vivid teals, and the rolling blanket of warm, cinnamon-toast sand. Even after all this time, it still brought a smile to her face to look at it. The soothing colors and tranquil scene never failed to relax her, no matter how stressful her day had been.

It made her feel she was somewhere safe. That she was home.

As she felt some of her cares melt away now, an idea kindled to life in her imagination.

An idea that would not only allow her to give something all her own to the beach house B&B, but also bring their guests a little tranquility or joy every time they looked at it.

With courage and inspiration swelling in her breast, she picked up her phone and called Annie.

"Hey, Hannah," her sister said in greeting. "What's going on? Is everything okay with Dad?"

"Yeah, everything's fine here, Annie. I, um, I have something to ask you about the beach house. You might think it's silly, though. And if you do, that's totally okay."

"I'm sure I won't think that. What's this about?"

Hannah told her what she wanted to do, then waited in nervous silence as Annie went quiet on the other end of the line.

"I think it's a great idea, Hannah."

"Really? You do?"

"Yes! I love it, in fact. Do you think you can get it all done in time for our opening?"

Hannah's heart started racing as fast as her imagination. "I know I can, but I'll have to get started right away."

"Okay, why don't you plan on coming to the house first thing in the morning, then? I was going to wait here for Gabe to arrive before I left for Noah's place, but if you're willing to be here at eight to let him in, I can pack up my things now and be with Noah starting tonight."

Hannah couldn't tell what Annie was looking forward to more, knowing the beach house would soon be ready for inspection, or her temporary relocation into Noah's place while the work was taking place.

As for Hannah, some of her enthusiasm dimmed at the reminder that in order for her current idea to work, she'd have to share the house with Gabe while he was there. Just the two of them. Working under the same roof for hours at a time.

She bit her lip in consternation. Maybe it would be better if she waited until he was finished before she added her personal touches to the house. Then again, if she waited too long she risked either having to rush, or not getting the opportunity to start her work at all before the B&B was open for business.

"Are you still there?" Annie asked.

"Yes, I'm here. Just thinking." Hannah blew out a slow breath. She refused to be hindered by the prospect of Gabe scowling and grumping around the beach house with her. "I actually have this week off from the gift shop, anyway, so I can be at the beach house early tomorrow to get started…and to wait for Gabe."

"That would be so great, Hannah. Noah's going to be thrilled when I tell him I can be at his place a bit earlier than planned. If you need anything while you're at the house tomorrow, just call me, all right?"

"I will. Go enjoy your time with your fiancé. I've got this."

They ended their call and Hannah sat on the edge of her bed, torn between excitement and apprehension. She would simply have to make the most of the situation. After all, she had charmed more than her fair share of overheated, mood-soured tourists in her line of work at the Gift Emporium. Surely, she could handle being cooped up for a few hours a day with a dull stick-in-the-mud like Gabe Lawson.

Shaking off her negative thoughts and misgivings, Hannah reached for one of her sketchbooks. Then, with a sense of renewed purpose and hope, she began filling one sheet after another with all of the visions that were springing to vivid life in her mind.

CHAPTER 6

Gabe rose with the sun that morning, eager to start his first full day of work at the beach house. Showered and dressed in a comfortable pair of jeans and a light-blue T-shirt—another concession to Henry's cajoling about his drab wardrobe choices—he stuffed a granola bar in his pocket for the drive and swigged the lukewarm dregs of his cup of instant coffee before heading out to his truck to make his 8 a.m. appointment.

It turned out his rental cottage was just a quarter-mile walk down the beach from the Taylors' house, but the drive took about fifteen minutes. The town of Crestpoint Beach had expanded and evolved over time, and consequently there were few straight shots from one point to the other. Gabe navigated through the network of narrow neighborhood streets crisscrossing the residential area along the coastline until he rolled into the driveway of the big blue-and-white Victorian.

With his tools and other gear in both hands, he walked around the house to the side that faced the sparkling water and the soft, sugary sand. He paused there for a moment and glanced up at the home that had been entrusted to his care.

He wasn't a sentimental type, but he took pride in his work and he never forgot for an instant that every job he worked on was something more than that to the people who hired him. In Hannah and Annie's case, this house was not only the foundation of their futures, but it was also a cherished piece of their past. He felt the weight of his responsibility settle on his shoulders as he walked up onto the veranda and rapped on the screen door's frame.

The interior door was open behind the screen, and he could hear the faint sounds of pop music playing somewhere inside. A female figure with blonde hair emerged from one of the first-floor rooms to approach the door.

Gabe had been expecting Annie, but it wasn't her coming to greet him.

He felt a scowl forming on his face as his brain registered Hannah's curvy, petite shape and the perky way she walked. Today she was wearing a pair of light denim overall shorts on top of a sunshine-yellow tank. Her thick, spiraling blonde waves were gathered back in a ponytail that bounced behind her with each energetic step she took.

She smiled as if she didn't notice he was frowning at her. "Good morning, Gabe."

"Hi, Hannah." She pulled the door open for him and he stepped inside. She held a coffee in one hand, the scent of vanilla, cream, and dark-roasted beans wafting toward him from the paper cup. "Are you and Annie ready for me to get started today?"

"We sure are. Except Annie's already relocated temporarily to Noah's place, so you're stuck with just me today."

"Oh." Maybe there was a more polite response he could

have chosen, but as he set down his things and watched her pivot away and sail toward the kitchen, all he could think about was how in the world he was going to concentrate on anything as long as Hannah was in the house with him.

She picked up a second paper cup from the counter and brought it to him. "Coffee?"

"Sure. Thanks." The thought of something other than instant was too hard to refuse.

"I hope you like caramel. I didn't know what you'd like, so I got you the same thing I have."

He actually preferred simple black coffee over the fancy concoctions that were so popular now, but she didn't need to know that. Her thoughtfulness made him willing to try anything.

As he took the steaming cup from her, their fingers brushed momentarily. The natural pink in Hannah's cheeks went a little brighter, and he tried to ignore the zing of electricity he felt as their gazes held for that brief moment.

He was here to work, not ogle.

He took a sip of the sweet, vanilla-laced coffee. "Whoa, that's pretty good."

"Coast Coffeehouse," she said, smiling over the rim of her cup. "Best brew on the beach."

He returned her smile and took another drink. "All I've got at my rental is a jar of instant, so this is a treat. Thanks again."

"No problem."

She was so pretty, her blue eyes so warm and inviting, it was hard keeping his eyes off her, especially when she was standing this close to him. To keep from staring, he sent his gaze traveling around the house. "Well, long day ahead. I should get started. I'm sure you have other things you'd like to do, rather than stick around here while I'm making a lot of dust and noise."

"Oh, I won't mind. I've got some music going upstairs."

He turned a questioning look on her. "You're going to hang out here today?"

"Actually, I'll be working here all week."

"You will?" He didn't like the sound of that, and it probably showed in his stiff reply.

She nodded, taking a sip of her coffee. "Don't worry, I'll try to stay out of your way."

He didn't see how that was going to be possible when his work was going to take him all over the house. The idea of bumping into Hannah while he was trying to focus was bad enough, but he also didn't need to be worrying about her safety while he was banging around.

His frown came back again. "What are you going to be working on?"

She bit her lip, tilting her head. "Want to see?"

"Sure."

"Come on." She motioned for him to follow her, then led him up to the second floor.

The music he'd heard when he arrived was originating from one of the guestrooms. It was louder up here, playing over a pair of small speakers she'd connected to her phone. As they entered the guestroom, Hannah hurried over and turned the volume down on the dance tune from the Seventies.

"Sorry," she said, blushing a little as she turned to face him again. "Big ABBA fan here."

"Noted." Gabe chuckled in spite of himself. "I prefer a good country song myself, but each their own."

He looked past Hannah to the wall behind her. What had been a blank field of neutral beige paint when he'd toured the house yesterday now bore the rough, penciled outlines of a sketched mural and the first splashes of color in the upper left corner of the composition.

"You're an artist?"

"Not really," she answered, looking sheepish now. "I dabble just for fun, that's all."

He stepped closer to her work, which depicted a whimsical, tropical scene with a lighthouse in the background and a cute mermaid dominating in the center of the mural. At the moment, most of it was merely penciled-in outlines, but he could tell the end result was going to be something vibrant and unique.

"Is that the lighthouse here in town that your dad used to manage?"

"Yep," she said, her face beaming. "That's the one."

Gabe nodded, turning his head to study more of her composition.

"You probably think it's cheesy, right?"

"Not at all." He shook his head, glancing at her. "It's fun. I think it'll really bring this room to life."

Much like the woman herself, he had to admit. She stood in a soft wash of morning sunshine that came in from the window, but her smile and beautiful face were the true light in the room.

"I'm going to paint something different in each of the guestrooms, so they all have their own vibe. There'll be a couple of serene murals for folks who come here looking for relaxation, and the rest of the rooms will have brighter themes. In the background, they'll all incorporate some of the other landmarks and attractions around town."

"Clever," Gabe said. "And very creative."

"You think so?"

"I do. Not only will your murals make your guests happy while they're staying here, but they'll also help the B&B stand out from all of its competition."

She smiled warmly. "I hadn't really thought of all that, but I guess you're right."

Even though she'd demurred when he asked if she was an artist, he could tell she was passionate about her work. He recognized that look in her eyes because it mirrored his own. As open-hearted and free-spirited as Hannah was, there was also an intensity about her when she was talking about her art.

He could have stayed and talked with her about it some more, but getting lost in those big blue eyes of hers wasn't going to make his workday any shorter. "Well, I should get started downstairs and let you go back to your work up here, too."

"Oh. Okay," she said, her smile dimming a bit at his abrupt non sequitur. "If you need anything, just give a holler. You might have to do that literally, because I like my music a little loud while I paint."

"I'll keep it in mind," he said, already stepping toward the door. "Thanks again for the coffee, Hannah."

"You're welcome, Gabe."

He left the room and headed back down to prepare for tackling the tasks he needed to complete today. First, he had to cover the furniture and floors, then he could start in on the real work. He'd made up a schedule right down to the hours it would take for each item on his list, determined to make the most efficient, best use of his time while he was working at the house.

If he stuck to the plan and didn't run into too many snags, he expected he'd be finished in under two weeks' time with all of the inspector's requirements and the accessibility updates Hannah and Annie had added to the list.

Since Hannah would be working in the bedrooms upstairs for however long it took her to paint her murals, he shuffled a few things on his workplan to keep himself occupied on the first floor to start. Fortunately, he had brought all of the tools and supplies he needed for the first-level bedroom and bathroom modifications, so he got started on that job before the others.

As he went back and forth between his truck and the house for one thing or another, he found himself smiling at the continuous stream of disco songs that filtered down from the second floor on a continuous loop. Although it wasn't his thing at all, the upbeat, playful music fit her. Once or twice, he even caught himself tapping his foot to the beat.

Hannah had promised to stay out of his way, and so she had, keeping to herself for the duration of the morning while he sawed and hammered and sanded the new doorframes for the first-floor bedroom and bathroom.

A question about some of the trim styles sent him upstairs to compare the baseboard he was working on, and as he reached the top of the steps, he couldn't resist peeking in on Hannah's progress. He found her working painstakingly on the mermaid, adding light and shadow to the fiery orange color of the siren's hair. Gabe stood utterly silent, respectful not to startle her while she worked. The truth was, he also wanted to steal a few moments and simply enjoy the sight of her doing something she so clearly loved.

Standing on her toes, Hannah added a few more touches to the mermaid's windswept locks, her strokes moving in time to the music blasting out of the speakers. She dropped back down to her heels and gazed up at the mural that was coming to life in vivid colors.

She must have sensed she wasn't alone, because in that next instant, she wheeled around and spotted him standing outside the door. She gasped and the paintbrush she held slipped out of her fingers. It hit her bare foot, leaving a streak of orange paint on her skin.

"Sorry," Gabe said. "I didn't mean to interrupt."

"No worries." Instead of getting upset, she laughed. Bending to retrieve her brush, she tried to wipe the paint from her foot but only made it spread. He noticed she had a smudge of blue on her chin, too. "I love painting, but it can be so messy."

Gabe chuckled. "Yeah, construction is the same way," he said, gesturing to all of the sawdust on his clothes.

Hannah smiled. "How's everything going down there? I hear a lot of racket, so I guess that's a good sign, right?"

"I'm surprised you can hear anything over that so-called music you're listening to."

"Was that a joke, Gabe Lawson?" She gave him a look of mock astonishment and he couldn't help but laugh along. She shook her head. "I'm going to forgive you for cutting on my musical tastes, but just this one time."

He couldn't hide his smirk. "I'll try to refrain from future commentary."

"Thank you," she said smartly, still grinning at him. "Hey, it must be about lunch time by now. I'm thinking about grabbing something to eat in town. Want to come with me?"

The invitation caught him off guard. The fact that he would have liked nothing better than to say yes caught him off guard even more. He didn't know what to make of their pleasant back-and-forth, but he was pretty sure advancing it into a lunch date was not a good idea.

He needed to pump the brakes on his attraction to Hannah Taylor, not give it more fuel.

"I, uh…I wasn't planning to take a break just yet. I'm on a pretty tight schedule here."

"Too tight of a schedule to eat?"

He scratched the back of his neck. "I usually just eat a snack and power through the day, especially on jobs where I'm working alone."

"You sure?" She looked crestfallen, even though her inviting smile remained in place. "There are easily half a dozen great places to eat only a few minutes away from here. It wouldn't take very long to go and come back."

"Maybe another time."

He didn't really mean that, and he could tell she was smart enough to see that fact. A small frown tugged at the edges of her mouth.

"Okay," she murmured. "I guess I'll just clean up a bit and head out, then. Want me to bring something back for you?"

"No, thank you, Hannah. I'm going to head back down and continue working now."

She nodded, then turned around and left him standing at her back while she turned off her music and began to clean up her paints. Gabe wanted to kick himself for the disappointment he saw on her face in the instant before she turned away from him.

He left the room in silence, telling himself it was better to nip his attraction to her in the bud, rather than make it worse by allowing Hannah to get any further under his skin.

This was only the first day of what was looking to be a very long week of working under the same roof together.

CHAPTER 7

A warm afternoon breeze blew the fragrance of wild roses and coconut sunscreen up from the beach as Hannah sat with Annie and their good friend, Zoe, a couple of days later at Daisy's Café, unwinding after enjoying a delicious lunch at one of the oceanfront eateries in town.

Hannah had been forced to take the day off from painting her murals at the beach house in order to let Gabe install the new handrail and balusters for the staircase.

It was probably just as well. In the two days they'd been working in the house together, they had hardly exchanged more than a handful of sentences. If she didn't know better, she'd think he was deliberately avoiding her.

Okay, she did know better.

He was totally avoiding her, and had been ever since she'd blurted out her invitation for him to join her for lunch.

"I mean, did he think I was asking him out on a date or something?" she complained to her female companions for what wasn't the first time. She stabbed her straw into the ice cubes at the bottom of her lemonade. "The way he's been acting around me now, you'd think I offered to paint a mermaid on his truck instead of politely inviting him to take a break from his work so he wouldn't starve all day."

Annie and Zoe laughed.

"Maybe he's just shy," Zoe said, her dark brown curls tumbling around her shoulders as she shrugged and leaned forward to sip her sweet tea.

"He's not shy," Hannah said. She thought of her brief interactions with him at the house these last couple of days and shook her head. "Gabe is confident and direct and intense. He's really funny, too. Or at least he can be, that is, when he's not busy scowling and stomping around like he wants to be anywhere else but under the same roof with me."

Annie lifted a brow. "Wow. You really do like him, don't you?"

Hannah let out an exasperated sigh. "Is it that obvious?"

Both Annie and Zoe gave her confirming looks. She sank her face into her hands on a groan. "Why did it have to be him? He hardly notices me, and when he does, he gets this deep furrow between his eyebrows then immediately goes back to hammering or sawing or tearing something apart."

"Hm," Annie hummed.

Hannah lifted her head. "Hm, what?"

"It seems to me that you might not be the only one struggling with an unwanted attraction."

Hannah scoffed. "I seriously doubt that."

"I think Annie may be right," Zoe added. "Do you and Gabe have anything in common?"

Hannah shrugged. "I hardly know anything about him, other than the fact that he works like a machine, he's a perfectionist about every little detail…Oh, and he hates my taste in music."

"Well," Annie said, drawing the word out. "He may have a point about the music."

Hannah playfully knocked shoulders with her. "Not you, too!"

A soft laugh broke from Zoe. "He doesn't sound all that bad to me. I've seen him, so I know he's not bad to look at, either."

Hannah sighed. "No, he's actually maddeningly handsome. Why couldn't we have hired a builder with a giant beer belly and a comb-over? Or anyone else at all?"

"We tried," Annie pointed out. "Gabe was our last and only hope. We're just lucky to have him, so try not to drive him off with your penchant for disco, all right?"

Hannah laughed, feeling some of her gloom lift the longer she sat with her sister and friend under the shade of the Daisy's covered deck. For a few minutes, she simply soaked up the tranquility of the cozy beachfront restaurant and the rhythmic roll of the waves nearby.

The three of them had finished eating a while ago, and as they chatted, their waiter swung by with the check. They split the bill and the tip three ways and paid in cash. Hannah had only been able to eat part of her oversized club sandwich and chips, so the remaining half was now packed neatly into a to-go box on the edge of their table.

At somewhere close to one in the afternoon, both Zoe and Annie had other places they needed to be. Zoe was due back at Seaside Designs, the home furnishings store where she worked, and Annie had plans with Noah and his sixteen-year-old daughter, Lainey, later that day after school let out.

As for Hannah, she could either head back home to her father's empty house while he was out at his weekly fishing excursion at the pier with a few of his buddies, or she could wander back to the beach house to check in on Gabe's progress.

She had never been good with idle time, and the only pressing thing waiting for her back home at the moment was laundry, so after saying goodbye to Zoe as she got into her car, Hannah asked Annie to drop her off at the beach house.

"You want to come inside with me and see how things are going?" Hannah suggested, hesitating as they parked in the short driveway on the street side of the house.

Muffled knocking sounds carried from within, where Gabe was evidently still hard at work.

Annie shook her head. "I'd rather be surprised at the big reveal. Between you and Gabe, I trust everything is going to look amazing in the end."

"Thanks," Hannah said, then leaned over and gave her sister a hug. "Tell Noah and Lainey hi from me."

"I will," Annie said. "Tell Gabe I agree with him on the music."

"Never," Hannah muttered around a laugh. "Love you, sis."

Annie smiled. "I love you more, Hannah Banana. Call me later."

Hannah nodded as she climbed out of the Corolla, waving to Annie with one hand and clutching her boxed lunch leftovers in the other. As she made the short walk around to the waterfront side of the house, she noted that the loud pounding noise had stopped.

When she rounded the corner and approached the steps up to the veranda, she found Gabe coming out through the screen door at the same time. He held a bottle of water to his mouth and had his head tipped back as he drank.

He didn't see her yet, and for some reason her feet stopped short in the sand and all she could do was stare as he downed half the bottle, the muscles of his biceps bulging below the short sleeves of his sawdust-coated black T-shirt. Heat rose in her cheeks and she knew she couldn't blame the afternoon warmth for the sudden lightheadedness that swept over her.

Gabe lowered his chin as he brought the empty water bottle away from his mouth and wiped the back of his free hand across his lips. A light sheen of sweat glistened on his skin. Errant strands of his glossy, dark hair were plastered against his forehead, making him look like a fairytale warrior fresh off the battlefield.

Hannah gaped, suddenly finding it difficult to breathe, let alone speak.

Gabe frowned. "Is everything okay?"

"Um, yeah." She nodded a bit too vigorously. "I heard you hammering something in here, so I thought you were still working on the staircase."

"I just wrapped up." He scratched at the side of his face, where a thin rivulet of perspiration trailed into the hint of dark whiskers shadowing his jaw. A rare smile quirked the corner of his lips. "I didn't expect to see you today. Or have you come to check up on me?"

"I'm not here to check you out," she said, then winced when she heard what came out of her mouth. *Check him out?* She wished for a sinkhole to open up under her and swallow her whole. Awkwardly, she held up the white to-go box. "Since I know you probably haven't eaten yet, I brought you half of a sandwich from Daisy's Café."

He glanced at the box. "I haven't been to that place yet. Is it good?"

"The best." Hannah walked up the steps and held the box out to him. "You haven't lived until you've tasted their club sandwich. It's beyond awesome. Full disclosure, I ate the other half for lunch, but I promise I didn't even touch what's in this box."

Since she couldn't even persuade him to eat fresh food with her, she didn't actually expect him to accept her leftovers, either. To her complete astonishment, he took the box out of her hand and brought it with him as he walked over to one of the Adirondack chairs on the veranda and sat down.

"Beyond awesome, huh?"

She nodded, taking a seat in the chair next to him. He opened the lid, his green eyes going wider as he peered inside at the sandwich that was piled high with turkey, ham, and bacon, plus fresh lettuce, ripe tomatoes, and a perfect dollop of seasoned mayonnaise.

He glanced at her. "Wow, this does look amazing. Thank you."

She smiled, waiting with anticipation as he took his first bite. As he chewed, he closed his eyes and moaned—actually moaned—with unabashed enjoyment. It was the first time she'd ever seen him let down his guard and truly indulge in something, and she couldn't deny that she was fascinated.

"It's good, right?"

"Incredible," he murmured, then went in for another taste.

"You're going to need more water if you keep wolfing that down so fast."

She got up and dashed inside to get a couple of bottles out of the refrigerator, if only to give herself a few moments to catch her breath. The sight of the updated staircase with its beautiful new balusters and polished wood handrail made her heart skip almost as much as this new side of Gabe Lawson.

When she went back out, he was still eating, his gaze fixed on the turquoise water that stretched out to the horizon.

"Here you go," she said, setting one of the waters on the flat armrest of his chair.

"Thanks." He glanced at her, and instead of looking away in the next instant, his gaze lingered. "It was quiet around here without you today."

She wasn't sure if he was simply making a statement or saying something more. His steady stare put a nervous flutter in her stomach. "I'm sure you were relieved to not be subjected to my superior musical preferences."

He smirked. "I didn't miss that, no."

Hannah swallowed, afraid to ask if there was anything about her that he *had* missed. It would be completely inappropriate to flirt with him, no matter how hard it was for her to resist. He had been nothing but professional since he'd started working on the beach house. Just because he was eating a sandwich she gave him and looking at her without a frown creasing his brow didn't mean Annie and Zoe were right in assuming he shared any bit of the attraction she felt toward him.

Still, it was nice sitting next to him on the veranda while the warm ocean breeze skimmed over them and sent her seashell wind chimes dancing lightly on their strings. She had never seen Gabe in a state of calm inactivity, least of all when she was anywhere near him.

"The stairs and balustrade turned out beautiful," she said, anxious to fill the silence while he continued eating the sandwich and chips.

"Thanks," he replied. "I tried to find spindles and a

handrail that were similar to the house's original. I know you and Annie want to preserve as much of the historic character as possible."

Hannah nodded, touched that he would take such care on their behalf. "Your choice was perfect. Have you worked on a lot of Victorians?"

"Only a handful. Back in Denver, most of the work my business partner and I took on was new construction residential properties and some commercial buildings, so this is a treat."

"I'm glad you're enjoying it."

She hadn't heard him talk much about his life in Colorado, let alone mention his business partner. She recalled that when she had asked him about it that first day he arrived at the beach house, he'd curtly informed her that the nine-year partnership hadn't worked out.

In fact, judging from the way he'd spoken about it, she had gotten the feeling that the split had been much worse than he'd let on.

"Do you keep in touch with anyone back in Denver since you moved here?"

He took a drink of water before answering. "I've got a few friends I've stayed in contact with. My sister, Sabrina, lives there, too."

"Oh. Is she older than you, or younger?"

"Two years older, but she's always acted like there are ten years between us."

Hannah laughed. "I can relate. Annie's only five years older than me, but she's been a kind of surrogate mom since our own mother died when I was three."

Gabe looked at her, his expression almost tender. "I'm sorry, Hannah."

She lifted her shoulder. "It's okay. It happened a long time ago. The worst part is not being able to remember much about my mother."

"How did you lose her?"

"Breast cancer. She was sick for more than a year, which was really hard on everyone else more than me, since I was so young."

He nodded solemnly. "My mom's been gone ten years now. She went quick—heart attack—but I don't think there's any easy way to lose someone."

"No, there's not," Hannah agreed. "I'm fortunate that I had Annie in my life after our mom was gone. Sounds like you're close with your sister, too."

"Yeah, Sabrina's great. The hardest thing about making the move to Crestpoint Beach was knowing I'd only get to go back and visit her once or twice a year, depending on my workload."

"What about your dad?" Hannah prompted. "You mentioned he's retired back in Denver, right?"

"We're not close," he replied tightly. At first, Hannah thought that's all he was going to say. But then he exhaled a heavy sigh and leaned forward, his forearms resting on his thighs. "My parents split up when I was in ninth grade. Dad worked a lot of long hours on construction projects, and Mom was a nurse. Things were…combative between them a lot of the time. Finally, they divorced. Sabrina and I moved in with Mom, and we didn't see much of our dad until his injury."

"What happened to him?"

"About fifteen years ago, he fell off a beam at his worksite and broke his back. He's been in a wheelchair ever since."

"How awful," Hannah gasped. She'd never given that much

thought to the hazards of what Gabe or his father before him did for a living. The idea that one misstep could not only end a career but permanently alter their lives, too, put a knot of worry in her chest.

Gabe leaned back in his chair. "My pop's a stubborn cuss who never accepted help from anyone, even when he was younger. That only got worse after his accident. When it started becoming obvious that he couldn't take care of himself on his own anymore, Sabrina and I moved him into a nursing home last winter. I don't think he'll ever forgive us for it."

Hannah couldn't keep her hand from coming to rest lightly on Gabe's shoulder for a moment. The feel of his firm muscles beneath her fingers was impossible to ignore, but she only meant to offer him a gesture of comfort. "I'm sorry," she said. "Maybe your father will come around one day to realize you and your sister were only trying to look out for him."

Gabe scoffed quietly. "Yeah, maybe. I'm not going to hold my breath on that, though."

He went back to eating for a few minutes, his gaze returning to the beach and the crystalline waves lapping at the shore. A flock of pelicans soared across their view, before dipping low and hitting the surface of the water like dive-bombers.

Gabe made a low sound of amusement as he watched one of the birds pop back up to swallow its catch while it floated on the gentle surf. "I didn't think I could enjoy looking at the water as much as I love the mountains, but I have to admit, this isn't a bad view."

Hannah smiled. "I've never been anywhere but here. Someday, I'd love to see the mountains."

"You'd like them, I think. There's a life-affirming comfort

in seeing something that immense and unshakable. It's reassuring, in a way. No matter how badly your world seems to be crumbling around you, those mountains are holding steady, just like they have been from the dawn of time and will be long after we're gone."

Hannah wondered how often he'd looked to his mountains for the kind of reassurance he described. His parents' divorce had obviously been tough on him. His father's injury and resulting estrangement didn't seem easy for him, either.

If she had to guess, she imagined whatever had happened between him and his business partner had deeply impacted Gabe, too.

"Do you think you'll ever move back to Colorado?"

He gave a firm shake of his head. "That part of my life is behind me, now. I needed to start over somewhere new after having my business torn right out from under me."

"What happened? If you don't mind me asking, that is."

He glanced at her, and although that frown she'd gotten used to seeing on his face was starting to form as he held her gaze, it faded. Something shifted in his eyes as he looked at her. "No, I don't mind telling you. It's embarrassing, though. Humiliating to think I was so trusting, I didn't even suspect my partner was robbing the company blind."

Hannah gasped. "Oh, no."

"Oh, yes," Gabe murmured. "Wyatt Cavanaugh and I were good friends for years. We met on a job site and it didn't take long for us to start talking about teaming up on a firm of our own. We were both hungry for success, and neither of us was afraid of the hard work it would take to build a competitive company in a city like Denver. For several years, everything was great. Our contracts were coming in almost faster than we could handle. I loved working in the field, but Wyatt decided one of us should focus solely on bringing in new business and managing the projects we had. He took over the scheduling and the books, freeing me up to supervise our crews and make sure every job we took on exceeded the client's expectations."

"It sounds like it was the perfect partnership," Hannah said, even though she already knew the eventual outcome had been anything but perfect.

Gabe nodded. "I thought it was. Wyatt gave me no reason to doubt it. But then, out of the blue, I learned our payroll didn't clear the bank. Wyatt seemed to be ignoring my calls and texts, so I got in touch with the bank and they told me the firm's checking account had less than two thousand dollars in it. The savings account was empty, too. It turned out, Wyatt had been draining the company dry in order to fund his gambling addiction. Just like that, everything we worked for—everything I worked to achieve—was gone."

Hannah closed her eyes and slowly exhaled, unable to imagine the horror Gabe must have felt at the discovery of that awful news. Now, she understood why he was so serious about his business. His stiff, impenetrable exterior had come from being burned by someone he thought he could trust.

"I'm so sorry, Gabe."

He smiled with wry resignation. "Live and learn, right?"

"So, here you are, starting over in Crestpoint Beach."

"Yep."

"Do you have a lot of clients?"

"You're the first."

Her brows rose. "In that case, we'll have to be sure to give you rave reviews."

He chuckled. "All kidding aside, I'd really appreciate that. It's not going to be easy landing large projects and hiring a reliable crew as the new guy in town. Particularly when it'll mean having to explain why my last business failed. Any way I slice it, the reason for the failure stops right at my door. I should've paid closer attention. Because I didn't, our clients and crews suffered, too. People's homes were delayed. Employees' wages were owed. I'll be paying back the balance of those debts for another twenty years unless I can get things off the ground here."

Hannah gaped at him. "You're repaying what your partner stole? Most people in your position would go bankrupt and try to move on."

"My pride wouldn't let me do that. One lesson my father drilled into my head from the time I was a kid was to never accept failure. Besides, I couldn't let anyone else suffer for Wyatt's actions or my blindness to them. I had a nice nest egg saved up over the years, so that took care of the bulk of the problem." He shrugged as if it was no big deal that he'd shouldered the responsibility all on his own. "So, I have to make do for a while. At least, my conscience will be clean when it's over."

Hannah didn't know what to say. She had sized him up all wrong.

Gabe Lawson wasn't a dull, standoffish grump. He had layers she'd never imagined. He'd suffered losses similar to her own—worse, in fact. Yet, he bounced back. He stood tall and took steps to make things right, even if he hadn't been the one at fault.

He was honorable and good.

And, yes, he was heart-stoppingly handsome, too.

Her awareness of him as a man made the warm breeze feel

even balmier as it gusted softly through the veranda. She wanted to touch him again.

She wanted to kiss him.

Instead, she folded her arms in front of her and watched as he finished off the rest of the sandwich in a couple of bites.

When it was gone, he turned a satisfied grin on her. "Thanks again for the sandwich, Hannah. You were right—beyond awesome."

"You're welcome, Gabe."

He dusted the crumbs off his hands and stood up. "Well, I've still got several hours of daylight left, so I should get back to work."

"Oh, okay."

Hannah rose, too, suddenly face to face with him, only a foot separating them in the shade of the covered porch. For a moment, neither of them said a word. Hannah stared up into his eyes, feeling as if she were truly seeing him for the first time.

The way he looked at her made her heartbeat quicken and her breath feel too shallow in her lungs. She parted her lips to get more air and his gaze drifted to her mouth.

Anticipation crackled between them, almost too much for her to bear.

Then Gabe blinked and took a step back, as if the physical closeness to her was more than he intended. He cleared his throat. "The uh...stairs aren't quite ready for a lot of traffic yet, but they'll be fine if you want to come inside and paint some more on your mural."

"Sure," she murmured, forcing a casual smile. "That would be great. I'm so close to finishing the first mural, I've been itching to get back to it so I can start another."

His expression went deadly serious, and he held up his index finger. "On one condition."

"What's that?"

"We alternate the soundtrack for the rest of today. One hour of my music for every hour of your…whatever you want to call it."

She tipped her head back and laughed. "All right, Lawson. You've got a deal."

CHAPTER 8

*G*abe should have extended his music demands through the rest of the week.

As he tapped the last nail into the new porch rail on the veranda two days after he'd struck his deal with Hannah, he chuckled, pausing to listen to the song she seemed to favor above the dozen others she tended to play on endless repeat. For all his grousing and complaining, he actually didn't despise her music nearly as much as he let her believe.

How could he, when it was obvious how much joy it brought her?

At the moment, he could hear her singing along with the tune, belting out the lyrics about a teenage girl who was on the dance floor, having the time of her life. He wasn't sure when Hannah Taylor had gone from unsettling distraction to endearing confidante, but there was no coming back for him now. Their talk on the veranda a couple of days ago had only driven home what Gabe already knew.

He liked her.

He more than liked her. He wanted her, and if he wasn't careful, those feelings for her could become a big problem.

Baring his soul to her over the best sandwich he'd ever eaten didn't change the fact that she was still his client.

Still, it was impossible to work under the same roof with her and not be drawn to her. Setting down his hammer, he entered the house and headed up the stairs to look in on her progress with the mural. She had finished the mermaid painting yesterday morning, and had since moved on to a different guestroom where she'd decided to paint a soothing mural of the sandy dunes that were a popular feature of Crestpoint Beach.

The music swelled as he got closer to the second-floor room where she was working. She had no chance of hearing him over the song that had her dancing in place in front of her mural, paintbrush held to her mouth like a microphone.

Today she wore a royal blue T-shirt over a pair of loose-fitting white denim shorts. Paint smears marked the back of her shorts. More specks of soft greens, yellows, and blues spattered her long, tan legs and bare feet. To Gabe, the vibrant woman in front of him was as much a work of art as the mural she was bringing to life on the wall.

He leaned against the doorframe and smiled, observing her from behind with a mix of amusement and desire as she rolled her hips and shoulders to the beat while she sang with unabashed pleasure. A few spiraled strands of her pale blonde hair tumbled out of her messy bun as she moved and sang, immersed in her own world.

It wasn't until she suddenly twirled on her bare feet that she noticed he was there. A bubbly laugh burst out of her, lighting up her entire face. Lord, she was beautiful. Especially when she turned that high-beam smile on him.

"How long have you been standing there?" she shouted over the music.

He chuckled. When he answered, he deliberately kept his voice low. "Long enough to lose my heart to you."

"What?" She held up her finger, then grabbed her phone and muted the speakers. Her cheeks were flushed a pretty pink, her blue eyes sparkling with happiness. "I couldn't hear you. What did you say?"

He smirked to himself. "I said I just finished the veranda railing and I'm going to start on the porch steps next."

"Oh." She propped her fists on her hips and gave him a thoughtful look. "You're going to be finished before you know it."

"Yeah, I think you're right." He shrugged, acknowledging to himself that the prospect of wrapping up the project didn't hold as much appeal as it did when he'd started. "There's still a fair amount left to do, though."

He was making decent progress on the long list of tasks on the inspector's report, however, there was still plenty of work ahead. By his estimations, he had only made it past the halfway mark on the list, and the clock was ticking if he wanted to ensure Hannah and Annie were approved for business by their deadline.

To that end, while picking up dinner one night, he'd run into another contractor in town and got to talking with him. The builder offered his assistance if Gabe needed another pair of hands in order to finish ahead of schedule, but he was reluctant to bring on anyone else who was unproven. Gabe kept his number, but he was intent on finishing up the beach house on his own. It was his first project, and he was going to be the one to get it done right.

He also wanted to get the place as close to perfection for Hannah as humanly possible.

Her pert nose scrunched as she stared at him. "What time is it?"

"Around noon, I guess."

"I'm starved," she said. "Want to break for some lunch?"

His automatic denial sat on his tongue and refused to budge. Was it really only a few days ago that the idea of pausing his work to indulge in Hannah's company had been completely out of the question for him?

Lately, he found himself making excuses to bump into her while they worked, or to ask her opinion of one thing or another, simply for the chance to talk to her.

As much as he might want to deny it, he was starting to fall fast and hard for this woman.

"Actually, you know, I could probably do with a short break," he said. "Where do you want to go eat?"

"How about on the beach?" She plopped her paintbrush into a container of water and cleaned off her hands on a damp cloth beside it. "I'll pack us a picnic."

Her answer took him by surprise. "Sounds good, but all I have to contribute are a couple of protein bars."

"Of course, you do." She playfully rolled her eyes. "I'll handle the food. There's a picnic basket in the storage room near the back door of the house. You go fetch that, and I'll find some things to fill it."

"Okay, boss."

They headed downstairs together, Gabe jogging off to carry out her instructions while Hannah made a beeline for the kitchen to wash her hands and gather their lunch items.

When he returned with the flap-top wicker basket, he found Hannah in the process of assembling a couple of turkey sandwiches. Packages of meat and sliced cheese from the local deli lay open on the granite counter, while she was rinsing a head of romaine lettuce.

She shot him a wry look. "I have to warn you, my sandwiches pale in comparison to Daisy's Café."

Gabe smiled. "You aren't going to hear me complaining."

"Good," she said. "Want to grab that tomato out of the fridge for me?"

"Sure." He set the picnic basket down and retrieved the tomato. Hannah held her hands out and nodded for him to toss it to her. He gently let it go, grinning as she smoothly caught it and brought it under the running water. "Nice skills. You play baseball?"

"No, but you should see me juggle."

He laughed. She did, too, slanting a warm look at him as he leaned his back against the counter at her side. "We'll need some waters."

"On it," he said, digging a couple of bottles from the refrigerator.

As soon as he had put them in the basket, she gave him another order. "Beach blankets are in the hallway linen closet near the bathroom down here. Bottom shelf."

"Anything else?" He asked, after he'd returned with a teal-and-white plaid blanket and set it next to the basket.

"I think we've got everything," she said.

With the two sandwiches halved and tucked into plastic zipper bags, she put away the ingredients and wiped down the counter. She added a bag of potato chips and a cluster of purple grapes to the feast, then opened the freezer and pulled out an ice pack.

"Ah!" she blurted, snapping her fingers. "I almost forgot dessert."

A small white box wrapped in pink-and-white baker's twine sat on the counter next to the fridge. She carried it carefully, packing it into the basket with the rest of their picnic. Another zipper bag containing some paper napkins seemed to complete the collection.

"Ready?" she asked.

"More than ready, now that I'm smelling all of this food."

He folded the blanket over one arm and picked up the basket in his other hand. Hannah gave him a questioning look, so he gestured forward with his chin. "You're in charge of finding the best picnic spot on the beach. I'm just the pack mule."

She smiled, then together they headed outside into the sunshine. It was hot, as usual, but Gabe had been getting acclimated to the warmth and humidity since he'd moved into the cottage up the beach. The almost constant breeze was a welcome presence, especially around midday.

Strolling alongside Hannah as she led them toward a place to sit down, he didn't think he would have minded if he was walking on the sun itself.

She paused on a flat plane of beach a few yards from the beach house. "How's this spot?"

"Looks good to me, but I'm no expert. This is my first beach picnic."

She gaped at him. "And you've been in town for nearly two months now? You are doing this beach life all wrong, Gabe."

"That's what my buddy Henry says."

"Well, he's right. Hand me the blanket, please."

He passed it to her, then set the basket down so he could help spread the blanket out. Hannah put the basket on one corner, then uncovered some smooth rocks buried in the sand and used those to weight down the other corners.

"Tip number one of beach picnicking," she said. "Don't let your blanket blow away."

Gabe chuckled as they sat down in the middle of their square dining area. "Glad I wore shorts today," he remarked, wiping his forearm across his brow. Hannah was staring at him, a cryptic smile on her lips. "What is it?"

"Your shirt," she said, pointing to the bright peach T-shirt he'd thrown on over his khaki cargo shorts.

He glanced down at the shirt he'd reluctantly bought on Henry's advice. "Is it frying your retinas, too?"

"No, I like it." She sank her teeth into her bottom lip as she shook her head, making some more of her curly waves escape her messy bun. "It's nice to see you in something other than black or gray or military green. You'd better watch out or people are going to start thinking you're a local."

"That doesn't seem like such a bad thing to me."

"Does that mean you think you'll be staying in town for good?" She glanced away from him as she asked the question, busying herself with the basket. "That first day you came to the house, you said you weren't sure about making things permanent in Crestpoint Beach."

She pulled out the sandwiches and handed him one. Gabe let his fingers brush against hers, a touch he was more than willing to steal.

"I want to stay," he admitted, realizing just how deeply he meant it. Staring into her eyes made him never want to leave the spot where he was sitting right now.

"Do you think you'll be able to build your business here?"

"I'm going to give it all I've got."

Her smile seemed shy, a rarity for Hannah. She dropped her gaze. "I hope you stay."

So did he. In fact, he couldn't think of anything he wanted

more than to stay in Crestpoint Beach and spend more time with Hannah. There were countless things he wanted to say to her, and he barely held them all in as he watched her now.

A gust rolled in off the water, unraveling her loose bun. Her hair tumbled free, some of it blowing into her face. Before he could stop himself, Gabe reached out and hooked a wild tendril behind her ear.

She glanced up at him with a look of surprise…and awareness.

He pulled his hand back, swallowing on a dry throat. "Could you pass me one of those waters?"

"Sure." She handed a bottle to him, her gaze searching his. "Would you like some chips?"

He nodded. "Chips would be great."

They ate in silence for a few minutes. He had to force himself to keep his attention on their surroundings, rather than the beautiful woman seated across from him on the small patch of fabric.

This wasn't a date, yet there was no denying it had the charged energy of one, especially after the way they had connected the other day on the veranda. Gabe wasn't accustomed to letting people into his personal life, yet he'd told Hannah everything. He'd only known her for a handful of days, yet he felt as comfortable around her as if she had been part of his life forever.

He enjoyed the time he spent with her, and he didn't want to think about how quiet and colorless things were going to be once his work on the beach house was completed and he had no reason to spend time there anymore.

Hannah would be gone even earlier than that, in fact. She was painting her murals during the week she had off from work at the gift shop. In a few more days, he'd be working alone at the house. While that might have given him reason to rejoice in the beginning, now it only made him wish he could slow time down.

He took a bite of his sandwich, then followed it with a drink of water while he tried to ignore the longing inside him. "I've been meaning to tell you, Hannah, your murals are coming along really well."

"Thanks." She popped a grape into her mouth, giving him a shy smile. "They're actually turning out better than I'd hoped. I can't remember the last time I felt so inspired by something I was working on. I'm going to be a little sad when they're finished."

He would be, too, but he kept that to himself.

"Do you know what you'll be painting in the rest of the guestrooms?"

She nodded. "In addition to the mermaid and the dune murals, there'll be a dolphin scene in one of the other rooms, a pelican design in another, and in the room where Annie and I used to sleep when my family lived in the house with our grandparents, I'm going to paint a nighttime mural with a sky full of stars and moonlight shining on the water."

All of her planned paintings sounded great, but it was clear that this last one meant something special to her. "What made you think of the night scene?"

Her gaze grew wistful. "Not long after our mom died, Annie used to sneak both of us out the window of that bedroom so we could sit on the rooftop and gaze at the stars. I remember her sitting with her arm around my shoulders while she pointed to each of the constellations and we tried to guess which star was our mom shining down on us. Those are some of my best, earliest memories. I'll never forget them as long as I live."

Gabe listened, moved by the vulnerability in her voice, and the fact that she felt close enough to him to share the story with him now. "It sounds like you and Annie have a very special bond."

"We do. She's been a beacon to me all my life." Hannah paused, as if she wasn't sure she wanted to say more. She met his stare. "Sometimes Annie's light shines so bright I get a little lost in the shadow of it, but that's on me, not her."

"What do you mean?"

"Annie's always been the ambitious one. Growing up without our mom, she was the one my dad and I turned to for everything. At eight years old, she had to be a mother to me and a helper to my dad. A lot of expectations were heaped onto her shoulders at an early age. That might've broken other kids, but it only made Annie stronger. She always had big dreams, and she went out and achieved them. I can't begrudge her anything, because I know how hard she's worked all her life."

"You make it sound like you haven't," Gabe pointed out. "I realize we haven't known each other very long but from what I've seen, you work harder than just about anyone I know. You've been looking after your father for years, in addition to working with the public day in and day out at the gift shop. I know that's not an easy job, even though I'm sure you make it fun for everyone who enters the place. Plus, you're an incredibly talented artist."

"Do you really think so?" She asked it with complete earnestness, as if she had no idea how truly gifted she was.

"Hannah, your paintings are just as good—better, I'd say—than a lot of the stuff I've seen in galleries in Denver. If you wanted to, you could take your art as far as your dreams can stretch."

She inhaled deeply, then let it out on a soft sigh. "That's the nicest thing anyone's ever said to me, Gabe."

"I'm only being honest."

"Thank you. Not only for your praise about my paintings, but for everything else you just said, too."

He only nodded in response because his voice was suddenly hard to find. He wanted to reach out and take her hand in his. More than anything, he wanted to kiss her.

He had never broken his rule about keeping his business life separate from his personal life, yet every minute he spent with Hannah shaved closer and closer to the edge of his control.

His heart pounded against his rib cage as he fought the urge to touch her.

His conscience told him he didn't have that right—not until she was no longer a paying client that his business depended on in order to get its foothold in a new town.

Even that was barely enough to prevent him from giving in to his feelings for her.

Instead, he leaned back, putting some extra distance between them.

Awkwardly, he cleared his throat. "Didn't I hear you say something about dessert?"

CHAPTER 9

Hannah's cheeks felt hot and ripe with color as she turned away from Gabe to reach into the basket. For one wild instant, she actually thought he might have wanted to kiss her.

Obviously, she'd been imagining things.

The noontime sun must be addling her brain. How else could she have mistaken his appetite for lunch and dessert for something else? *Her.*

"Do you like cupcakes?" she asked, still facing away from him as she dug through the basket.

"Who doesn't?"

She pulled out the bakery box and untied the candy-striped twine. "These are from my favorite bakery in town, Sweet on You. I picked them up yesterday and then forgot to take them home with me for Dad. Not that he should have them, anyway. Annie and I are trying to get him on a healthier diet plan."

Gabe smirked. "Too bad for Dad."

Hannah opened the lid and let him peek inside the box at

the four fancy, frosted cupcakes. They were all different, and each piled high with creamy icing and a variety of toppings. A couple of them were crowned with candy and colorful sprinkles. Another sported bright red cherries and drizzled chocolate syrup. The fourth one had a slice of candied lime wedged into the center of a fluffy cloud of vanilla frosting garnished with coconut shavings.

"Whoa, that is a sugar overdose just waiting to happen." He glanced up, grinning. "So, which one can I have?"

She laughed. "Take your pick. I love them all equally."

He opted for the chocolate-and-cherries. Hannah went for the coconut-and-lime.

"Is this really your first beach picnic?" she asked, trying to make light conversation to distract herself from watching him indulge in the sweet treat. She was already paying too much attention to his lips as it was.

He licked some of the gooey frosting off his fingers. "This is my first picnic, period."

Hannah stopped eating and stared at him. "For real?"

"Scout's honor."

"Don't people picnic in Colorado?"

"Sure, they do. If you don't mind fighting the local wildlife for your food."

Her eyes widened. "Local wildlife?"

"Yeah. You know, coyotes, mountain lions, bears." He slanted her a teasing look. "Don't worry, you only have to run faster than your slowest picnic partner."

"You're terrible." She leaned forward and playfully smacked his knee. "So, if you don't picnic, what did you do for fun in Denver?"

"There's tons for people to do there."

"No, Gabe. I'm talking about you. What do you do for fun?"

He had to think about it for a minute. Most of his adult life had revolved around construction, whether that was honing his skills as an apprentice for other people in his teens and early twenties, or putting in long hours and a great deal of sweat to build the business with Wyatt.

"The fact that it's taking you this long to answer worries me," Hannah lightly teased.

"I used to like hiking and climbing when I was younger."

"Climbing, as in…mountains?"

"Yeah. Colorado's got more than fifty fourteeners."

"Fourteeners?"

"Fourteen-thousand-feet elevations. I've climbed ten of them. Each one's about eight miles round-trip, but it'll take the full day and you've got to start around two or three in the morning because the storms tend to move in around the afternoon. Weather miscalculations can end up being as fatal as anything else on the mountain."

"That is your idea of fun?" Her eyes went wide. "I was expecting you to say you like making fancy cutting boards with your routing saw, or that you collect stamps when you don't have a hammer or a level in your hand."

"Cutting boards and stamp collecting?" He practically choked on his laughter. "I see I've made quite an impression. Do I really seem that boring?"

She arched her brows. "Not boring, exactly. Just… measured. You know, deliberate. Serious. Not someone who'd consider death-defying outdoor activities anything close to fun."

"Uh, huh. Boring."

She held her fingers to her mouth to cover her snicker. "That's your word, not mine."

He laughed along with her as he popped the remainder of his chocolate cupcake in his mouth. Hannah took another bite of hers, too, while a comfortable calm settled over them again.

Gabe took a swig of water, then skewered the bottle into the sand so it wouldn't tip. As he did so, something seemed to catch his eye near the edge of the blanket. "Hey, look at that."

He picked up a small white shell and held it in his palm. Hannah moved closer to have a look.

"Oh, that's a coquina shell. They're all over the place around here."

"Check it out," he said, holding it between his thumb and index finger. "There's a perfect little hole hollowed out of it right at the top."

Before she realized what he was doing, Gabe reached for the loose baker's twine she'd taken off the box of cupcakes. Threading one end through the hole in the shell, he fed it through the hole until the coquina reached the middle of the twine.

Hannah smiled as he held up the makeshift pendant. "Very nice."

"Come here," he murmured, gesturing for her to lean toward him.

She did as he asked, her heart fluttering like a swarm of butterflies in her chest. She lifted her chin and held still as he leaned close and reached around to fasten the ends of the twine at the back of her neck. This close, he smelled amazing. Warm, sun-kissed skin and masculine spice, mixed with the fresh ocean breeze and trace sweetness of chocolate.

His fingertips brushed her nape and she inhaled a shallow breath.

"Sorry," he said, his deep voice rumbling.

"It's all right."

His eyes shifted to meet hers. "Is that too tight?"

She shook her head, mute with the sudden clamoring of her senses. Bringing her hand up to touch the delicate gift he made her, she smiled. "It's perfect. Thank you."

She drew back, blinking at him slowly. Gradually, his eyes shifted down to her lips and then back up, his breath quickening. "You don't really have to wear it."

Hannah's heart galloped as he stared at her. No more than a few inches stood between them on the blanket now. She couldn't think of anything she wanted more than to close the space between them and feel his lips against hers.

So, that's exactly what she did. Without another thought, she moved toward him and pressed her mouth to his in a soft, unhurried kiss.

Gabe made a low, strangled noise in the back of his throat as his hands came up to tenderly hold her face as their kiss lengthened, deepened.

Hannah didn't know how long they stayed like that, their mouths joined and their hands gently holding each other. When they finally parted, she was out of breath, a dizzy smile on her face as she gazed into Gabe's heavy-lidded green eyes.

"Wow," he murmured, his voice low and raspy. "That was…"

"Yeah," she whispered, biting her lip, which still tingled from the feel of his mouth on hers.

That familiar furrow between his dark brows appeared, but he looked anything but annoyed as his eyes searched her face. He blew out a short breath. "Is it me, or did the temperature just soar about a hundred degrees?"

Hannah smiled. "Try a thousand degrees."

His mouth quirked. "That much, huh?"

She nodded. "Maybe we'd better cool off before the neighbors start to talk. Race you to the water?"

His frown disappeared, replaced by a look of surprise. "Swimming? Now? It's the middle of the day and I've still got work waiting inside the house."

She rolled her eyes at him. "Yes, and it'll still be waiting when we get back. Come on, Gabe. Live a little."

Before he could voice any further argument, she scrambled to her feet and took off running across the hot sand.

She wasn't sure he would follow, but when she threw a look over her shoulder, she spotted him tearing after her at full speed. Shrieking in delight, she darted as fast as she could for the water's edge.

Her bare soles slapped against the wet sand as she splashed ankle-deep into the surf. She hadn't even gotten out as far as her knees before a pair of strong arms wrapped around her from behind and lifted her right off the ground.

Gabe swung her all the way around before setting her down again. As soon as she was free, she reached down into the water and splashed him, wetting the front of his T-shirt and shorts. He retaliated, sending an arc of warm saltwater across her entire front.

"Ooh, now you've asked for it," she said, bending down to use both hands to lob her next assault.

He charged at her like a bull, sweeping her high into his arms once more before he let go and let her drop her into the thigh-high waves. She popped back up, drawing her hands over her face to clear the wet strands of hair that now hung over her eyes and around her shoulders.

She gaped at him. "I can't believe you just did that!"

A look of concern came over his handsome face. "Are you okay? Did I hurt you, Hannah?"

She didn't answer, waiting until he came close enough for her sneak attack. As soon as he was in firing range, she let loose with another round of relentless splashing.

"Oh, I see how you play," he shouted, trying to fend off the barrage of water warfare she was sending his way. He shook his head, sending droplets of water sluicing off his dark hair.

When he leapt toward her, Hannah pivoted on a giggle and tried to escape him.

She wasn't fast enough. He grabbed her around the waist, then dragged her back through the water until she was flush against him. He held her there, her spine pressed against the solid heat of his muscled chest as she struggled half-heartedly to break loose.

He set her down after a moment, but his arms stayed locked around her while they both laughed and the rolling waves crashed against their legs.

"You are trouble, Hannah Taylor," he said in a quiet voice beside her ear as he held her.

His grasp loosened, and he took a step back, allowing some space between them. She moved out of his reach, turning around to face him. As they stared at each other, the air seemed charged with intensity, almost too much to take.

Hannah wasn't sure if she wanted to escape the heady feeling that was building inside her, or if she wanted to grab it close and never let it go.

No, that wasn't true.

She knew what she wanted.

Him.

She didn't know when it happened, but she had fallen hard for Gabe Lawson.

She swallowed, wishing she had the courage to tell him everything she was feeling. But she couldn't tell if he felt the same, or if the past hour they'd spent on the beach was only a casual diversion for him.

What she felt was anything but casual.

She was falling in love with him.

Quite possibly, she already had.

"Gabe, I..."

He ran his hand over the top of his head, pushing his wet hair back and regarding her with a note of regret in his eyes. "This wasn't a good idea, Hannah. I think we should go back to the house now."

Some of the air left her lungs at the finality of his tone. Whatever had been happening between them this afternoon was clearly over now, and the all-business side of Gabe had returned front and center.

With one last look at her, he turned and started heading back to their picnic area. Hannah followed, wringing out her drenched shirt as she watched him march ahead of her with purpose.

Silently, they packed up the basket and shook the sand out of the blanket, then made their way back inside the beach house to continue their work.

CHAPTER 10

The end of Hannah's week painting her murals at the beach house came faster than Gabe was prepared for.

After the way he'd messed up their day of picnicking a few days earlier, he should have been relieved that the torture of sharing the house while they worked was finally drawing to an end. He had done his best to keep his distance from her, unwilling to invite a replay of the kiss that had left him completely knocked off-kilter ever since it happened.

Hannah seemed equally determined to avoid him. She showed up early each morning and went straight to work. There was no more teasing banter, no more coffees shared out on the veranda, no more cajoling him to take a break to eat something with her.

She still played her music while she painted, but she kept the volume low now. He hadn't heard her so much as hum along with her favorite songs, let alone belt out the lyrics while she danced and twirled to the beat.

She had entered his life like a blazing, rainbow-colored

supernova, and after only a week's time in his company, he had managed to dim her light to just a shadow of what it was before.

For that reason alone, he wished he'd never taken the job at the beach house.

He had strived to keep his relationship with her professional only, and he'd ruined everything when he let her kiss him.

To be fair, it wasn't as if he hadn't wanted to feel her mouth on his, too.

He still wanted that.

In the days since, he'd made about a dozen bargains with himself that all he needed to do was maintain a respectable distance until his work was finished and the contract he had with Hannah and Annie had been fulfilled. Then, maybe he could persuade Hannah to let him start over again, once he was no longer employed by them and his work was able to stand—or fail—on its own merits.

That was the deal he'd struck with himself. It had been easier to adhere to it before the reality of her leaving was staring him in the face today.

He was upstairs installing the new fire sprinkler system when he heard Hannah on the first floor where she'd been painting the last of the five guestroom murals since she arrived at daybreak. Based on the sounds filtering upstairs, it appeared she was packing up her things a bit earlier than he expected.

Gabe stepped off his ladder and made his way downstairs. As he rounded the curved newel post he'd installed days ago, Hannah came out of the wheelchair-accessible bedroom at the end of the hallway. She held a sealed paint can in one hand. Tucked beneath her other arm were the folded drop cloths that had been spread on the floor while she'd been painting.

"Taking a break?"

She held his gaze, a guarded look in her eyes. "No. I'm finished."

"The dolphin mural is done already?" When she nodded, he forced himself to smile. "That's great. Will you show me?"

It took her a moment to reply. "Sure. Let me set these things out on the veranda first."

Gabe walked with her, opening the screen door to let her step outside. He held it for her as she came back in, trying not to notice how good she smelled or how silky her blonde hair looked the way she wore it loose down her back today.

She led him through the house to the large bedroom where she'd been working. Gabe paused just inside and marveled at the joyous ocean scene she'd painted on the far wall. Under a serene pastel sunrise, a pair of porpoises arced out of the pale turquoise water, plumes of white fanning out from where they'd leapt out of the waves. A grove of palm trees rose from a corner of the beach, all of the elements creating a tranquil scene that was sure to bring a smile to all who viewed it.

"Amazing," Gabe said, never failing to be blown away by Hannah's talent.

"Thanks," she replied, smiling briefly before glancing away from him. "Tomorrow I go back to the gift shop."

"I know. The week went by pretty fast, didn't it?"

"I suppose." She let go of a sigh as she squared her shoulders. "I guess I should get out of your hair now."

He didn't say anything. The only thought banging around in his skull was the certainty that he was not ready to see her leave. Not from the beach house. Not out of his life, either.

"Do you have plans?"

She looked at him suspiciously. "You mean this second? I'm just going to head home. Probably catch up on all of the laundry that's been piling up while I've been over here. Why?"

He frowned, shrugging his shoulder. "I'm at a logical break myself. Maybe we should go out and do something to celebrate all your work."

"Celebrate?" She peered at him as if he were speaking in a foreign language. "You want to celebrate…with me?"

He understood her skepticism, especially when they'd barely exchanged ten words over the past several days. But he wasn't ready to let her go yet. Some desperate, admittedly undeserving, part of him wanted to prolong the inevitable by any means possible.

"What do you have in mind, Gabe?"

Since it was pure impulse that he was making the suggestion, he had no clue what to offer her. But then an idea took hold and he couldn't keep the smile from playing at the edges of his mouth.

"How about if I surprise you?"

Her dubious expression deepened. "What kind of surprise? Gabe, I don't know if this is a good idea…"

"I promise it will be. Do you trust me?"

It was a loaded question at this point, but she appeared to consider it at least. Some of her reluctance seemed to give way to the insatiable curiosity Gabe adored about her so much.

Confusion swam in her blue eyes. "Why are you doing this?"

He wasn't going to try to pretend he didn't understand the real question she was asking. "I'd like us to be friends again, Hannah. Maybe once I'm finished here and the B&B is ready for business, we can see if there's a chance for us to be something more than friends."

She swallowed. "I'd like that very much."

"Good." He exhaled his relief, feeling it all the way down to his bones. "That's really good to hear, Hannah."

She tilted her head. "So, where does that leave us right now?"

"About a half an hour drive away from your surprise." He smiled. "Are you ready to see what it is?"

She gestured to her T-shirt, shorts, and sneakers. "Am I all right to go like this?"

"You're perfect. Let's go."

Hannah grabbed her purse off the counter, while Gabe fetched his keys and phone. They locked up the house, then went around to his pickup and hopped inside. Gabe drove out of Crestpoint Beach, heading for another town a few miles away.

"Are we going bowling?" Hannah asked as they drove through Ridgewood, a small inland town with only a few attractions to its name.

Gabe shook his head. "Nope. Even if you guess right, I'm not going to tell you."

"You're no fun."

He chuckled. "So you've implied a time or two. Maybe this will change your mind."

He turned off the central street through town and headed for a large, boxy building that rose five stories high and sprawled nearly the length and width of the entire block on which it sat. Gabe had been to the place a couple of times with Henry. Now, he waited for Hannah to realize where they were.

She saw the signage on the side of the building and

swiveled an incredulous look at him. "Are you kidding me? You're taking me indoor rock-climbing?"

He grinned at her. "Surprised?"

"Yeah. I'm a little bit terrified, too."

"Don't be," he said, parking the truck and turning off the engine. "I'll be with you every step of the way."

"You're crazy," she said, her smile growing.

He smirked. "That sounds a lot better than boring. Come on."

They got out of the vehicle and walked together across the parking lot. Gabe barely resisted the urge to take her hand in his, but there would be time for holding hands after the house was finished. Based on her reaction to what he'd said back at the beach house, he could hardly wait to pound the last nail into the inspector's report and get on with courting Hannah properly.

"Do we need equipment or anything?" she asked, bouncing along at his side with renewed excitement.

"We rent everything we need inside." When they reached the door of the facility, he held it open for her then followed her into the spacious lobby.

A few minutes later, after signing their waivers and grabbing their rental gear, they headed past the front area into the climbing area. The steep walls towered over them, colorful footholds dotting the entire expanse all the way to the top. A few other climbers scaled the angled walls, gripping the ropes connected to their harnesses as they moved from one foothold to another.

"Woah," Hannah gasped, staring up at the walls and the people hanging off them.

Gabe knew the sport could seem pretty daunting at first, but he would make sure she was safe and secure at all times.

He guided her over to the back wall where there weren't as many people before stopping and turning to her.

"So, this device is an auto-belay," he explained, helping her slip into her harness and fastening her in. "It's going to ease you down to the ground whenever you're ready to descend, okay?"

"Does it ever…break?" Hannah asked, a slightly concerned look on her face.

Gabe gave her a comforting smile as he clipped her harness to the auto-belay. He placed her hands around the rope, pausing to hold his hands over hers to ease her nerves.

"As long as you clip in, you'll be just fine. I'll be right beside you, and the auto-belay won't let you hit the ground at full speed," he reassured her as he clipped himself in. "Just make sure you land on your feet."

He placed his hand on her back and guided her up to the wall, nodding to signal for her to grab one of the holds.

Hannah reached forward and placed her hand on a bright pink foot hold, turning to give him a smile. "Here goes nothing."

"Step up on that red one first, then grab that blue one," he instructed her, motioning to the foot holds.

Hannah placed her foot on the red hold and hoisted herself farther up the wall to grab the blue hold. She looked back at him with a mixture of excitement and determination in her eyes.

"Look at me!" she called down to him, suspended only twelve inches off the ground.

Gabe chuckled. "I'm looking," he replied, unable to see anything else when she was in the room. He sent her a pleased smile before climbing up beside her. He was glad to see her having a fun time, despite only getting a foot up the wall. He couldn't imagine how thrilled she'd be when she got close to the top.

"What now?" she asked, raising an eyebrow at him as he climbed up next to her.

"Lift your foot to that one," he told her, lifting his chin to indicate another hold.

Hannah nodded and climbed up another foot, waiting on him to catch up before speaking.

"Think I've got the hang of it now."

"I think so, too. You're a natural."

She giggled like an exuberant child. "See you at the top."

Gabe watched her scramble higher. He moved with her, enjoying her playful competitiveness. Still, the protective side of him tensed as she pushed herself forward.

"Come on!" she urged from a few feet above him.

She reached for one of the holds, but her hand slipped. She gasped as she fell, the rope and harness catching her and the auto-belay easing her back down the wall toward the ground.

When she came close enough to him, Gabe reached out and hooked his arm around her back, letting go of the foothold so that he could drift back to the floor with her. Once they touched down, he steadied her, taking hold of her free hand with his.

"You okay?" He checked her over, hoping the fall hadn't scared her too badly. He had slipped plenty of times, both outdoors and on simulation climbs like these, and he knew the first ones were more than a little jarring.

"I'm fine," Hannah insisted, undeterred. "I want to go back up."

Her cheeks were flushed with color, both from the fall and the fun of her first climb. She was beautiful under any circumstance, but the way she looked at him now, with her head tipped back and her lips slightly parted nearly took his breath away. How he was able to resist kissing her, he had no idea.

"All right," he said, mentally shaking himself back to the task at hand. "If you're ready, let's go again."

A grin spread over her face. "This time, I'm going to make it all the way to the top."

Boosting off one of the holds, she started climbing up the wall again. Gabe watched her go, noting that she'd paid attention to his instructions and was taking on this challenge the way she took on everything else in her life—with exuberance and fearless confidence.

The only thing he'd seen her show uncertainty toward was her art, and he hoped one day she'd conquer that lack of faith in herself. He wanted to be the one at her side while she walked that path, the one she turned to for encouragement and support.

He wanted to be for Hannah what she was becoming for him. His light. His touchstone. His heart.

"You coming?" She called from a few feet above him, a daring smile on her lips. "Come on, Lawson. What are you waiting for?"

He chuckled. "I'm just giving you a fair head start before I blast past you."

"Game on," she shouted, her laughter ringing out as she reached for another hold on the rock wall.

They climbed for another couple of hours and by the end of the session, Hannah was keeping pace with him as if she'd been doing it for years.

As they drove back to Crestpoint Beach, she chattered animatedly, reliving her triumphs on the wall and laughing over her handful of missteps. Gabe didn't think he could ever tire of hearing her voice lifted with excitement and bubbly energy.

Some of her eagerness faded as they arrived at her house and Gabe parked in the driveway of the little white bungalow. He wasn't nearly ready for their time together to end, either.

"So, tomorrow I start back to work at the Gift Emporium again," she murmured. "It's going to seem strange not walking to the beach house every morning."

Gabe nodded. It was going to seem strange not having her there with him, too.

According to his task schedule, he still had about five days of work before everything on the punch list was checked off and completed. He was on track to bring the project in on-time, but looking at Hannah and knowing she couldn't be his until he was finished made him impatient to be done.

Looking at her from across the truck's cab, he wanted to camp out at the house and work twenty-four hours a day in order to wrap things up as quickly as possible.

"Maybe I'll pop in on you sometime this week," he said.

She stared at him, her hands moving restlessly in her lap. "And after this week?"

"We can talk about that then, all right?" He could hardly keep from reaching out to take her hand in his. The only way he did was because he knew if he touched her, then he'd also want to kiss her again.

He wanted that even without touching her.

"Hannah, what happened that day we had our picnic was a mistake—not because I didn't want to kiss you, because I did. I still want to kiss you, but I won't. I don't make a practice of blurring the lines between my professional life and my personal one. Right now, you're a part of both, and that's a problem for me."

She drew in a shallow breath, her eyes soft with apology. "You've become a big part of my life, too. I'm sorry if I've made things difficult for you."

He scoffed lightly. "You've made things difficult from the moment I laid eyes on you."

"I have?" The trace of a smile edged her lips. "So, where do we go from here, Gabe?"

"If it's all right with you, we're going to stay friends until your house is no longer in my hands. Then I'm going to ask you out on a proper date and we can start on sorting out the rest."

She nodded. "Okay. I guess I can deal with that."

Gabe wished he had some of her resolve. If she remained next to him any longer, he wasn't so sure he could keep his word. "Now, you need to stop looking at me so sweetly, so I can let you get out of this truck without caving to my desire to kiss you goodnight."

She laughed softly. "All right, if I must."

Pivoting, she reached for the door handle, then paused to look over her shoulder at him. "I want you to know that I've had the best time with you, Gabe. Not just today, but this whole past week."

He smiled. "Yeah, me too."

"Goodnight," she said, then eased out of the cab and shut the door behind her. She gave him a little wave before dashing up the sloped concrete driveway to the bungalow's front door.

Gabe waved back. He didn't let go of the breath he was holding until she had disappeared inside. Then he put his truck in reverse and drove back to the beach house to work for a few more hours.

CHAPTER 11

Laughter echoed through the dining room of Noah's cozy home a couple of evenings later, as Hannah helped Annie carry in the dinner they'd made together.

Sixteen-year-old Lainey was seated at the table with her dad and her boyfriend, Mason, while Hannah and Annie's father regaled everyone with some tall tales about his recent fishing exploits at the town pier.

"I tell you, the way that king mackerel put up a fight, I thought he was going to pull me right over the railing."

The kids' eyes went wide with amazement as Frank Taylor spoke. Hannah smiled fondly at her father as she set down a platter of baked chicken and vegetables.

"Okay, Captain Ahab, that fish story gets bigger every time you tell it."

He chuckled at her teasing. "Just because you didn't see it doesn't mean it didn't happen."

Hannah gave the teens a wry look and playfully rolled her eyes. "Is anyone hungry?"

"I am," Lainey and Mason said at the same time, then burst out laughing together.

Annie came into the dining room behind Hannah, holding a big bowl of fresh salad in her hands. "Do we have everything we need?"

"I think so," Hannah replied, smiling as she caught the loving look her sister and Noah shared across the table.

It had been a long time since they'd all gathered together, and there was a lot to catch up on. Everyone had ventured down their own path, building their lives together or alongside each other. Yet, no matter how busy life kept them, their connection to one another always seemed to draw them close, strengthening the bonds they were forming as a family.

Tonight's gathering only made Hannah more keenly aware of how much she missed Gabe.

She felt better about their relationship since their talk a couple of nights ago, but it didn't make the waiting any easier. She'd never met anyone with his work ethic or his personal code of honor. While she respected him for both, she also yearned to see him again.

As dinner continued on all around her, she couldn't help but watch Noah and Annie as they laughed together and stared into each other's eyes, so clearly in love. The look she saw on her sister's face was the way she felt whenever she was with Gabe, too.

She couldn't tell herself she was merely on the way to falling in love with him; she'd already tumbled in head over heels. Part of her wanted to believe that he felt at least a little bit of that same feeling for her.

More than once during the meal, she caught herself reaching up to touch the coquina shell necklace he'd given her. She'd taken it off after their picnic on the beach, partly because the baker's twine it floated on was delicate and kept coming undone. Mostly, she'd been reluctant to wear the gift because after their kiss and the walls he'd put up afterward, she'd left that day in a state of confusion and doubt about everything between Gabe and her.

She didn't have those doubts anymore. She was ready to give her heart to him completely. Once the house was finished, she hoped there would be no more walls between them.

Her thoughts circled back to Gabe time and again while she enjoyed the company of her expanding family and the dinner they shared. After the plates were cleared away and the dishes washed and put away, Hannah and her dad said goodbye to everyone and drove home for the night.

As they passed the beach house on the way to her father's bungalow on another street, Hannah noticed Gabe's truck was parked outside. Her heart leapt in her chest, even while she worried to see he was still working when it was going on nine p.m.

Her father shuffled off to bed soon after they got settled inside the house, but Hannah was too restless for sleep. Her mind was buzzing with the many conversations she'd had with Annie and Noah, and thoughts about the progress being made in the final stretch of updates on the beach house. More than that, however, she couldn't stop thinking about Gabe.

With her dad snoring peacefully in his bed, she slipped out of the house and made the short walk to the beach. It was a beautiful, clear evening. The night sky sparkled with countless stars overhead and the glow of a delicate crescent moon.

As she rounded the corner of the beach house and looked up at the veranda, she discovered she wasn't the only one admiring the twinkling constellations.

Gabe stood at the railing, taking a rare break and staring out at the stars. He held a white ceramic mug in his hand. Hannah could smell the aroma of strong black coffee wafting toward her on the light breeze.

"Hannah," he said, surprise in his deep voice. "It's late. What are you doing here at this hour?"

This was the first time she'd stopped in to see him since her last day painting her murals. She hoped her visit now wasn't unwelcome.

"I could ask you the same thing. Do you mind if I come up for a few minutes?"

"Of course, not. It's your house, after all."

She walked up the steps, which were sturdy and solid now that he'd replaced them. The veranda railing looked better than ever, too. "Looks like you're making great progress."

He nodded, holding up his cup of coffee. "I'm a man on a mission. I wanted to work as long as possible tonight and push through a few more things on the list."

"How much longer do you think you'll need before you finish everything?"

He smiled, probably because he knew the real question she was asking. How much longer would they have to wait before they could have that proper date he'd promised her?

"If everything goes well, I should be done in another five days. Less, if I keep myself heavily caffeinated."

Hannah laughed and moved in beside him at the railing. "Isn't it beautiful out here tonight?"

"Mm-hm. I used to think the night sky was amazing when I was in the mountains, but it's really spectacular here. The sky seems endless with the water rippling beneath it."

"This isn't even the best way to view them." An idea struck

her as she glanced at him. "You want to stargaze for a few minutes from the best seat on the entire beach?"

He considered for only a moment before a grin tugged at his lips. He set down his mug and nodded. "Sure, why not?"

Hannah led him up to the bedroom where she'd painted her mural of the starlit heavens. Just as she and Annie had done years ago, she lifted the window that opened onto the second-story rooftop. Gabe climbed out first, pausing to offer his hand for support.

Hannah took hold of him, even though her body instinctively recalled just how to navigate the sometimes slippery, angled slope of the roof. They found a spot to sit, their arms brushing as they settled back and got comfortable.

"Wow, you were right," he murmured, tipping his head back to look up at the sky. "This is an incredible view."

"I'm glad you like it, too."

They both went quiet, their eyes aimed high above. The breeze riffled her loose hair, and she drew a deep breath of fresh ocean air into her lungs.

After a few minutes, Gabe's low voice rumbled softly beside her. "Did you ever decide which one of them is your mom looking down on you?"

Hannah's heart squeezed to realize he'd remembered what she told him. She leaned toward him and pointed up so he could follow her finger as a guide. "You see that star right there near the Big Dipper? The one that looks a little brighter than the others around it?"

"I see it," he murmured, his warm breath skimming against her cheek.

"That's her. That's my mom, Ginny Taylor. I'm sure of it."

When she glanced at Gabe, she realized just how close their faces were. It hadn't been intentional on her part, but now that she was staring into his steady gaze, she couldn't seem to tear herself away.

He gave her a tender smile. "She must be shining so bright up there because of her pride in her daughters. Especially you, Hannah."

When she started to shake her head in denial, Gabe reached out and cupped her cheek in his palm. For a breathless second, she thought he was going to kiss her. She prayed he might, despite their agreement to remain friends for the time being.

Instead, he tilted his head down and touched his forehead to hers. The sigh that left him sounded heavy with restrained control.

A low, amused sound left his mouth. "You're wearing that silly necklace I made for you."

"I am. And it's not silly to me. I love it, Gabe."

He drew back a little, but his touch remained on her face. "I noticed you'd taken it off after that day we spent on the beach."

"The string is delicate. I didn't want it to break."

"I thought maybe you took it off because of me. The way I acted after our kiss."

She shrugged lightly. "That, too."

"I'm sorry." He frowned. "I should've talked to you about it, rather than trying to pretend that kiss didn't mean anything to me."

"It's okay. We're talking now. That's what matters more." She brought her fingers up to his jaw, unable to resist touching him when his hand still lingered against her cheek. "Now, I'm never going to take your necklace off ever again."

He gave a low chuckle. "In that case, I'll have to replace that baker's twine with something more permanent."

"I like the sound of that."

He smiled and his hand moved around the back of her neck. He started to draw her toward him. As he did, his fingers caught in the string of the necklace and it broke loose.

Hannah gasped as she felt the tiny shell slip off her neck. "Oh, no."

She attempted to catch it, but it slipped past her fingers. She heard it clatter onto the sloped roof, then begin to tumble down toward the edge.

"I'll get it," Gabe said.

He lunged forward, reaching out to grab for it. His momentum didn't stop.

The soles of his work boots scrabbled for purchase, but gravity worked against him.

Panic exploded in Hannah's breast as he began to fall. "Gabe!"

She thrust her hand out to him, but he refused to take it.

With a shocked-sounding breath, he tumbled off the roof and hit the ground below with a heavy thud.

CHAPTER 12

A high-pitched ringing sound filled Gabe's head as he rolled onto his back in the sand, his left shoulder throbbing with pain.

For a few seconds, he forgot what happened, the agony in his shoulder making his memory hazy as he tried to make his vision stop swimming. He felt something small and cool in his hand, prompting him to uncurl his fingers. Through his bleary gaze he saw the white coquina shell in his palm.

He groaned.

The fall replayed in his head and he closed his eyes, mentally berating himself for his clumsiness. At the same moment, he heard Hannah rushing out of the house and down the veranda steps in a panic.

He grimaced as another jolt of pain hit him. The ringing in his skull was still there, coupled with a pressure that made his head feel as if it were caught in a vise.

"Gabe, are you all right?" Hannah's concerned voice came from just above him. "Don't move, okay? Just stay still."

He couldn't form an answer at the moment, other than

another low moan. Despite landing in the sand, which was soft on the surface, he had evidently come down on his shoulder. The way his head was pounding, he had a feeling his skull had taken the hit, too.

Hannah's worry hurt worse than any physical pain he was feeling. He tried to push himself upright if only to reassure her that he was okay. The instant he attempted to sit up his vision spun as if he'd just spent an hour riding a tilt-a-wheel.

He dropped back onto the sand, feeling helpless and foolish. "I'll be all right."

"I'm not so sure about that." Hannah's touch was tender and careful as she brushed his hair back off his sweat-dampened brow. "I'm going call for help."

He let out another groan, but this time it was more out of humiliation than pain. "Don't. I just need a minute to catch my breath."

He opened his eyes and stared up at two of her hovering over him. Both Hannahs frowned, their beautiful faces pinched with fear.

"I'm calling an ambulance," they informed him in warbly stereo.

All he could do was lie there in self-directed anger as Hannah took her phone from the pocket of her shorts and made the call. Distantly, he heard her tell the dispatcher what happened and where she was. She answered a few more questions, her replies clipped and anxious.

"Okay. I will. Thanks, Denise," she said, apparently knowing the 911 dispatcher by name. "Please tell Matt and the guys to hurry."

Hannah's fingers lit gingerly on his forehead. "Paramedics are on the way, Gabe. Just hang in there, okay?"

Gabe felt almost numb, the pain starting to turn into a

dull, constant ache that wouldn't let up. He could hardly think straight because of it. All the while, Hannah stayed at his side, offering him comforting words and reassurances that he was going to be just fine.

Before long, a siren sounded on the beach road behind the house. Flashing lights lit up the night as the wailing siren grew louder and the rumble of the ambulance's engine growled.

"They're here," Hannah told him. Then came the rapid pound of booted feet on the short sidewalk leading out to the beach.

Gabe opened his eyes and watched as two paramedics and a good-looking fireman around Gabe's age jogged through the sand toward Hannah and him.

"Thanks, Matt," she said to the fireman.

"No problem," he answered, obviously on friendly terms with her. "We came as quickly as we could."

The guy's light brown hair had a surfer look to it, and he gave Hannah a warm smile as he and the two other men moved in to do their thing.

"Stargazing on the roof tonight, huh? Nice for that." The fireman named Matt knelt next to Gabe in the sand. "How're you doing? Any neck pain?"

"No," Gabe murmured quietly. He drew in a breath and hissed. "My shoulder—"

"Yeah, it looks like you did a number on that," Matt replied. "How about your head? Are you dizzy? Do you feel like you're going to vomit?"

"No. I hear ringing, though. And there's some pressure behind my eyes."

Hannah's concerned look deepened into stark fear. "Is he going to be okay?"

Matt nodded. "Yeah, he will. Rick, you want to get the gurney? He's not going to be walking out of here on his own just yet."

Gabe groaned in protest. "I don't need a gurney. I'm fine, I just need another minute."

"Please, stay put," Matt said. "We're going to get you taken care of."

They were acting like he'd been in a car accident or something equally extreme. All he'd done was take a tumble off a roof, which was embarrassing enough, especially for someone who worked in building and construction.

The fact that Hannah had to see him being treated like an invalid only worsened his humiliation.

The paramedic came back pushing the gurney. Once it was in place, Matt grabbed one side of Gabe as the two other first responders grabbed his other side. After a quick countdown, they lifted Gabe onto the gurney.

"All right, let's load him up and get his shoulder looked at," Matt said, before grabbing the gurney and assisting in hauling Gabe back to the ambulance.

Curious people from a few of the neighboring beach houses had gathered outside to gawk at the fool who was being wheeled away from the scene of his utter chagrin. By morning, the news would no doubt have circulated all over town.

So much for making a good first impression on the community where he hoped to build his reputation as a trustworthy, responsible businessman. Now, he was going to be a laughingstock.

Hannah followed alongside the wheeled gurney, her gaze fraught with worry. She stopped behind them as they carried

Gabe into the back of the ambulance and got him situated for the ride to the hospital.

"Can I come along, Matt?"

"Yeah, sure." He patted the bench next to him. "Hop in."

Hannah thanked him before climbing inside of the ambulance and taking a seat next to him. She reached out to touch Gabe's arm, but drew her hand back when he winced as the vehicle lurched into motion.

Gabe swallowed, attempting to scrounge up whatever pride he had left, but it was hard to do that when he felt so disappointed in himself. He was always careful and aware of what he was doing. He thought things out before he did them. He never took unnecessary risks.

Tonight, his recklessness not only endangered himself, but Hannah, too.

He didn't really care about his own pain as he looked up into her distressed face.

What if she had been the one to fall instead of him?

He didn't even want to contemplate it.

One of the paramedics checked Gabe's vitals while the ambulance rolled through town.

"Can you tell me your name?" Matt asked.

"Gabe Lawson."

"What's your date of birth, Gabe?" When he gave the answer, Matt moved on to the next question, and then another one after that, the interrogation no doubt designed to make sure he hadn't rattled loose anything more than his pride when he took his spill.

All the while, Gabe could only look at Hannah and be thankful it wasn't her lying on the gurney in his place.

He was forced to relive the whole episode for her friend the fireman, who seemed to be trying to keep him alert and talking when all Gabe wanted to do was shut his eyes and sleep.

Not that the agony in his shoulder would give him peace enough to do that. Every bump and jostle made pain arc through him.

"What's our ETA?" Matt asked the paramedic behind the wheel.

"Five minutes."

"Gabe, how are you doing?" Hannah asked, her voice breaking through the noise in his head. "You look pale."

"I'm fine," he muttered.

"They'll give you something for the pain when we get to the hospital," Matt told him, before giving Hannah a reassuring nod. "He'll be okay."

"Are you sure?"

"I promise."

Gabe turned his head to look back up at the ceiling of the ambulance, wishing he was anywhere but in this situation. His head pounded, but he was more troubled by his shoulder.

Any downtime for him meant all work stopped on the beach house. He had been working ahead of his own timeline, but he couldn't afford any delays if the place was going to be finished in time for the inspector to take another look and approve it to open for business.

His fall tonight may have just derailed all of Hannah and Annie's plans for being ready to book their first B&B guests by Memorial Day.

He had made them a promise, yet because of one act of irresponsibility on his part, the woman who meant everything to him might end up paying the price.

Gabe didn't know how he would ever forgive himself if he cost Hannah the dream she was working so hard to achieve.

CHAPTER 13

*H*annah walked alongside the gurney as Matt, Rick, and Jason wheeled Gabe into the hospital's emergency room entrance. As a lifelong resident of Crestpoint Beach, she'd known all three of the first responders for years, and it helped alleviate some of her worry knowing Gabe was in capable hands.

They wheeled him into the ER, then carefully placed him on a bed inside a curtained patient area to wait for treatment.

"Someone will be here in just a minute to take care of you guys," Matt said. "Gabe, good luck. Hannah, it was nice seeing you."

"You, too, Matt. Thank you."

He and the other men departed, leaving Hannah alone with Gabe in the semiprivate examination room.

"You're going to be okay," she told him, needing to hear it for herself as well. "I'm going to be right here with you the whole time."

"No." His face pinched and he gave a faint shake of his head. "You don't have to stay, Hannah."

"Where else do you think I want to be?" she asked as she gazed down at him, her heart squeezing with worry and affection.

She brushed her fingers lightly through his hair, hating to see him suffer. She blamed herself for the agony she saw in his face.

If only she hadn't stopped by the beach house tonight.

If only she hadn't coaxed him out onto the roof to look at the stars.

If only....

Her head was full of things she wished she had done differently. For all of her impulsiveness and spontaneity, this was the first time anyone had gotten hurt because of her.

That it was Gabe lying in agony in the emergency room only drove the sharp edge of her guilt even deeper.

He seemed unwilling to even look at her now, turning his head on the thin hospital pillow and staring at the posters and containers mounted to the wall.

After a few moments, the curtain whisked open and a gray-haired doctor stepped behind it. Hannah recognized her family's general physician and breathed a sigh of relief.

"Hi, Doctor Miles," she said.

"Well, hello, Hannah. My goodness, it's been a while." He chuckled good-naturedly. "I suppose that's a good thing under the circumstances, right?"

She smiled and glanced at Gabe to reassure him. "Doctor Miles has been taking care of me and my family since I was a little kid. He'll patch you up in no time, I'm sure."

Gabe only grunted in acknowledgment, his pained eyes seeming to have a bit of difficulty focusing as the doctor leaned over his bedside.

"So, Gabe, let's have a look at you, shall we?"

"I think my right shoulder might be dislocated," he murmured.

"Hm." Doctor Miles's brown eyes peered at him in sympathy as he carefully examined Gabe's arm. "Yes, it certainly is." He took out a penlight and flashed it at Gabe's eyes. "Hit your head pretty hard, too, did you?"

"Yeah. I think so."

Hannah worried her lip, praying he was going to be okay.

Doctor Miles made a contemplative noise, then turned to Hannah. "Your friend's going to be just fine, but I'm going to have to ask you to wait outside while we reset his shoulder and run a few tests for his concussion."

"Concussion?" Hannah drew in a sharp breath, fighting the sob that suddenly lodged in her throat. "Oh, Gabe. I'm so sorry."

He scowled. "Do what the doctor asked, Hannah. Please."

His tone was clipped, and she didn't think it was simply the pain talking. He was upset.

He had every right to be, of course. He'd told her to stay away until he finished working on the beach house, but she hadn't listened. Selfishly, she'd gone to him tonight because her need to see him had evidently been more important to her than his stated wish to focus on his work.

Now, he was flat on his back in agony and with a head injury.

Hannah had never felt so small, or so miserable with herself, in all her life.

Doctor Miles gave her a compassionate smile. "I'll come out and update you when we're finished here, okay?"

"All right." Left with little choice, she slipped out of the curtained room so Gabe could receive the treatment he required.

She paced the waiting room, her heart in her throat. It felt as though she'd been in there for hours before the ER doors swung open and Doctor Miles strode toward her.

"How is he doing?"

"He's resting now. He'll be fine, Hannah. The shoulder will give him some discomfort for a while yet, but the worst of it was over once I popped it back into place. He should be able to treat it at home with a few weeks' rest and over-the-counter pain medication as needed."

A few weeks of rest. Hannah didn't want to consider what that meant, not only for the progress on the beach house, but for Gabe's business prospects as well. Knowing him as she did, mandatory idle time was going to be difficult for him to comply with. She would just have to make sure he took things easy, and didn't push himself to get back to full speed too soon.

"What about his concussion?"

The doctor nodded soberly. "I'm sure he'll recover without any issues, but I'm going to keep him overnight for observation just as a precaution. He should be well enough to be discharged in the morning."

Hannah swallowed, anxiety clawing at her. "Can I see him now?"

Doctor Miles gave her an uncomfortable look before he slowly exhaled. "I'm sorry, Hannah, but you'll have to stay out here. Gabe's recovering in his room. He's requested no visitors."

"But I'm not a visitor," she blurted, confusion and hurt twisting inside her. "I'm his…I'm his friend."

"He said he wanted to rest alone for the duration of the night. I'm sure he'll feel a lot better tomorrow, after he's had a chance to recuperate a bit."

Hannah felt as if she had just been run over by a train.

Gabe refused to let her see him. He was shutting her out again, except this time it felt different than when he'd avoided her after their kiss on the beach.

This time, the wall he was constructing between them felt taller, steeper.

It felt like a door closing in front of her face while she stood there.

She nodded woodenly, forcing a smile she didn't feel. "I'm sure you're right, Doctor Miles. I should let him rest. I'll just wait until tomorrow to check in with him once he's home."

The kindly old doctor gave her an understanding smile. "I'm told you rode in with the ambulance tonight. If you need a ride back and you're willing to wait a few minutes for my shift to end, I'd be happy to drop you off on my way home."

"Thank you," she murmured. "I'd appreciate that very much."

She hadn't even considered how she would leave the hospital when she'd left with the paramedics. Her only concern had been Gabe and getting him the medical attention he needed. She hadn't imagined she'd be leaving him overnight, let alone that he would bar her from his room.

She paced the hallway while she waited for the doctor to finish his rounds, then she rode in silence for most of the short trip home to the bungalow.

As they pulled into the driveway, she noticed the living room light was on, despite the late hour. Hannah felt a new sense of guilt, realizing her father was probably worried and wondering where she'd gone for so long tonight. She should have texted him to let him know what happened.

Now, she had someone else to apologize to.

"Tell Frank I said hello," Doctor Miles said as she climbed

out of his sedan and thanked him for the ride.

She waved goodbye to him, then quietly entered the house. The TV went silent, followed by her father's shuffling footsteps as he came out of the living room to greet her. His gaze lit on her with tender concern, as if he already knew where she'd been.

"Was that Doug Miles's car in the driveway?" When Hannah nodded, her father walked up and briefly gathered her into his embrace. "Ruben called a couple of hours ago after Jason told him about the patient they treated over at the beach house tonight."

"Oh, of course," Hannah said as it dawned on her that the paramedic was the son of one of her dad's card night buddies. "I'm sorry, Dad. I should've called you myself. Everything just happened so fast."

"That's the way it goes with accidents," he said, brushing some hair out of her face. "I'm glad you're okay."

"I'm fine."

"And your friend, Gabe?"

She shook her head, fighting back the emotion that clogged her throat. "He got hurt pretty bad tonight. His shoulder was dislocated and he's got a concussion. Doctor Miles says he'll be okay, but he's keeping Gabe at the hospital until tomorrow for observation."

"Ah, honey. I'm sorry."

"It's all my fault." The whole awful incident replayed in her mind as she followed her father into the kitchen and took the seat he pulled out for her at their small dining table. "After you and I came home from dinner tonight, I saw Gabe's truck over at the beach house and I decided to go see what he was doing working so late. We started talking about the stars, and I invited him up to the second-floor roof for a better view."

"Hm." Her dad sat in the chair beside her, nodding at her mention of the rooftop stargazing. "Your mom and I spent many a night up there together, too. Nothing compares to that view, especially when you're sharing it with someone you love."

"You and Mom used to stargaze from the roof of the beach house? When was that?"

He scratched his cheek, a glint of youthful mischief in his eyes. "Ginny invited me up there with her the first time when we were sophomores in high school. We hadn't started dating yet, but I had a crush on her like you wouldn't believe. We were supposed to be studying, but Ginny had a daredevil streak in her—rather like someone else I know," he said, winking at Hannah. "We climbed out her bedroom window onto the roof and spent the next several hours talking and watching the stars glitter above us. That was only the start. All through our courtship, that roof was our special place."

Hannah smiled. "Did Grandpa Joe and Grandma Betsy know what you were doing?"

"Oh, I imagine they did, but they let us have our fun. Ginny's parents were always kind to me. Lord knows I needed their support while she was sick, and later, after we lost her."

"You never told me this story before," Hannah murmured. "I never knew that bedroom used to belong to Mom."

He nodded. "Annie tells me you've painted a mural of the moon and constellations in that room. I think your mom would be very pleased to know your B&B guests will be looking at her night sky when they stay there."

Hannah couldn't speak for a moment, moved to silence when she considered all of the history—and the love—that used to live in the old beach house.

"When Annie and I were little, after Mom was gone, we used to climb out on the roof together, too. We'd search for her in the sky, trying to guess which star was hers."

His throat worked as he reached out and covered her hand with his. "Ginny used to whisper to you girls as she tucked you in at night that she would always be watching over you, even if you couldn't see her anymore. I guess she was right."

"Dad..." Hannah choked back her tears, feeling as if her heart had been cracked wide open tonight. Not only because of Gabe's terrifying fall, but now, hearing all of these new revelations about the past her father had shared with her mom, and the years Hannah was too young to remember, yet carried deep in her soul.

It was almost more than she could bear.

Her father patted her hand, his gaze tender on her. "I get the sense that you and Gabe have something special going on between you, too. Am I right, sweetheart?"

"Yes," she admitted quietly, then shook her head. "I don't know anymore. I thought so, but after tonight...I've ruined everything, Dad."

"What do you mean?"

"I'm to blame for his accident tonight. If I hadn't brought him up there, he wouldn't be in the hospital right now. Because of me, he's not going to be able to use his arm for several weeks. Possibly several months, according to Doctor Miles."

"If you're worried about getting the beach house ready to open, we can figure something out. We'll find a way to make it work."

"It's not only the B&B that's at stake," she said. "Gabe came to Crestpoint Beach to start over. His business partner in Denver bankrupted their construction firm, so Gabe's been paying back the debt personally. He's trying to build a new business on his own, and now those plans are pushed back until he's healed."

Her father listened, nodding thoughtfully. "He sounds like a good man, Hannah. He must be, if he means this much to you."

"He is a good man, Dad. He means everything to me."

"You love him, honey?"

"Yes. And now he probably hates me for taking away everything he was trying to build with one stupid, reckless mistake."

"Some moments in life are more important than what we may think we need or feel we have to prove—to ourselves or anyone else."

"Not to Gabe. He's got his plans. He's trying to make a new life for himself and I've just put it all in jeopardy tonight."

"Don't be so sure about that, Hannah. Gabe's the only one who can decide what's truly important to him. He might surprise you."

"I'd like to believe that, but I'm not sure I can. He shut me out at the hospital, Dad. He told Doctor Miles he didn't want to see me." Regret tasted raw on her tongue. "I think I really messed things up between us tonight, and I don't know if I can fix it."

"Hm," her father replied, but there was a wise-looking smile playing at the corners of his mouth. "There's another story I never told you about your mom, sweetheart. Did you know we broke up the year before we got married?"

It shocked her to hear that. Her parents had been married at the young age of nineteen, which meant their breakup had to have occurred during their last year of high school. At that time, Hannah's mother had been Crestpoint High's star tennis player, while Frank Taylor was apprenticing at the town lighthouse.

"I thought you and Mom had been inseparable from day one," she said, slowly shaking her head. "What happened to make you break up?"

"It was the weekend before Ginny was playing in a big tournament in Tampa. We're talking about a really big deal, her chance to shine on a national stage. She'd been training so hard and I wanted to do something with her to celebrate everything she'd achieved. I wanted to be romantic, so I showed up at her house riding an old tandem bicycle and we rode out to the lighthouse where I'd laid out a picnic for us on the beach."

Hannah smiled, picturing the scene. "That does sound romantic, Dad."

"Well, it would've been. Before we reached the lighthouse, the old bike threw its chain and we both tumbled off. I knew Ginny was hurt, but it wasn't until I saw the way her ankle had twisted in the fall that I realized what I'd done."

"Oh, no." Hannah brought her fingers up to her mouth on a quiet gasp. "It wasn't broken, was it?"

"No, thankfully not." Her dad heaved a remorseful sigh, as if he still felt guilty after more than forty years. "It was a bad sprain, though. Enough to keep her out of the tournament."

"Oh, Dad. She must've been heartbroken to miss her big chance. I'm sure she didn't blame you for what happened, did she?"

"Well, she was awfully upset. We both were. The competition she'd been looking forward to for months was over before it began, and I was the one who cost her that chance." His mouth flattened with sadness. "We broke up, and Ginny focused on her physical therapy for the next few months.

Eventually, she was healed enough to play another big tournament—bigger than the one she'd missed. And she won."

Hannah exhaled the breath she didn't even realize she'd been holding. "She did? You both must've been so happy and relieved that she was able to get back on the court."

"Yes, indeed. All I ever wanted was for Ginny to be happy, even if she no longer wanted me to be part of her life."

"You mean, you were still broken up even after she won the next competition?"

He nodded. "I didn't see her for almost a year. She traveled that whole summer after we graduated high school, playing in one tournament after another. Her star was rising fast. I knew it would only be a matter of time before she was far out of my reach here in the hometown. So, when I heard she was home in between events, I worked up my nerve and I decided to go see her one last time. When I got to the beach house, she was just on her way out."

"Where was she going?"

"She was on her way to see me." He smiled wistfully, his gaze distant with the memory. "Ginny told me she had decided to quit the tournament circuit."

"What?" Hannah gasped. "I thought she loved playing tennis."

"So did I," he said softly. "She did love her sport, but after spending all those months traveling and competing, she decided it wasn't the life she really wanted. She told me there was something that meant even more to her than the career that would've taken her all over the world. She wanted to stay in Crestpoint Beach and raise a family…with me."

Hannah smiled and gave his weathered hand a warm squeeze. "What did you say to her? What did you do?"

He chuckled. "I told her there was nothing on this earth I

wanted more than her, and then I got down on one knee and I asked my sweet, beautiful Ginny to marry me."

Hannah's eyes prickled with tears. Despite knowing that her parents would only end up having fourteen years together before cancer took Hannah's mother away, she couldn't view their story as anything other than a happily-ever-after. Their marriage had been full of love and happiness, even though it had ended much too soon.

"Dad, thank you for sharing that story with me," she said, sniffling past her tears. "Thank you for sitting with me tonight and trying to make me feel better. My situation with Gabe is different from yours with Mom, though."

He caught her hand in both of his, sandwiching her fingers between his palms. "What I'm trying to tell you is that life is bumpy sometimes. We make mistakes. We hurt people occasionally without meaning to, even the ones we love more than anyone else in our lives. But things have a way of working out, if they're meant to be."

She knew he was only trying to help, but her parents had already been head over heels in love for years before the bicycle accident that pulled them apart. She and Gabe had barely gotten started getting to know each other before her carelessness made him push her away tonight.

Hannah's heart had no reservations when it came to loving Gabe, but that didn't mean he felt the same way about her. Now, she'd probably gone and ruined any chance she had with him at all.

Her father patted her hand. "Give Gabe some time to sort things out for himself. He sounds like a smart fella to me. I'm sure he'll come around eventually."

Hannah offered a wan smile. "Thanks, Dad."

She prayed he was right.

CHAPTER 14

The doctor discharged Gabe before noon the following day with orders to rest up, medicate if he needed it, and call the hospital if his concussion didn't seem to improve over the next one or two days.

As for doing anything strenuous, that was off the table until his shoulder had a chance to heal. Which, according to Doctor Miles, could take as long as twelve weeks.

Three months.

His livelihood depended on him being physically able to work. His body and his brain were the true tools of his trade, yet he'd risked both last night.

Shouldn't he have known better after witnessing what his father's jobsite accident had cost him? Gabe had always told himself it would never happen to him. He was more careful than the old man. He was cautious and focused, never took his eye off the job.

Last night, he saw how quickly it could all come crashing down.

Unfortunately, he wasn't the only one his carelessness had harmed.

Gabe sighed as he adjusted the black sling on his right arm and slumped on the sofa at his cottage. As if being grounded from any activity beyond a short walk or some mild stretches wasn't bad enough, his injuries would also prevent him from getting any more work done on the beach house.

He'd only had a few days' worth of tasks left in order to complete the project for Hannah and Annie, but now it would be weeks or months before he could return.

Unless he healed up at miracle speed, the window for getting the beach house finished, inspected, and approved ahead of the bed-and-breakfast's opening schedule plans was as good as closed.

Gabe's reckless slip on that rooftop had just set their business back by crucial, lucrative months. He may have even forfeited the entire season for them.

Groaning, he reached for the TV remote and muted the action movie Henry had turned on after he'd brought Gabe home from the hospital about an hour ago. Although his friend offered to stay a while and help keep him entertained, Gabe had declined. He wasn't in the mood for company and chitchat, even with his best buddy.

The only person he truly wanted to see was the woman he'd coldly sent away from the emergency room last night.

He'd been in agony when he asked her to leave while the doctor was treating him. Seeing her looking at him from his bedside with such deep concern and affection had only made him feel worse. He'd been upset with himself and guilt-ridden over the fact that it could have easily been Hannah who'd been injured instead of him. That thought still terrified him.

Gabe didn't know if it was pain or self-directed anger that

made him ask the doctor to deny Hannah from visiting him. Now that his head was a little clearer and his shoulder wasn't screaming from the dislocation, he'd had time to think about how it must have hurt her that he'd turned her away without excuse. The fact that she hadn't texted or called him since then only confirmed how badly he'd messed up.

But it was probably for the best—for her, anyway.

More than likely, she realized how he'd put them both in danger last night, too. She had invited him up to the roof to look at the stars, not to make a move on her. He had promised to keep things under control while he was responsible for working on the house, yet he'd pounced at the first opportunity he had to touch Hannah, or to kiss her.

If he had kept a tighter rein on his feelings for her, neither one of them would be suffering like they were today.

The blame for everything that happened last night rested squarely on him.

By now, Hannah had probably reached that same conclusion, too.

As much as he wanted to reach out to her and apologize for everything, he figured it might be best to simply give her space for a while.

He glanced to the end table next to him. His phone and medications lay there, along with a receipt from Slice of Paradise, which he'd used to jot down the name and number of the building contractor he'd bumped into in town last week. But it was something else on the table that caught his eye.

The small white seashell that had fallen off Hannah's necklace.

Gabe had caught it before he hit the ground, and it was still clutched in his fist when he'd been treated in the emergency room. His heart broke a little when he looked at it now. It had been a silly thing to give her in the first place, yet she'd worn it as if it had been a precious jewel. Would Hannah even want it back anymore?

He picked it up, holding it gingerly in his palm as memories of the time they'd spent together filled his mind. Her smile and her laughter. Those warm blue eyes that seemed able to look straight into his heart. Her soft, sweet lips, and her kiss that made him long to promise her the moon and all the stars.

Right now, he couldn't even promise her that her house would be finished on time.

Gabe blew out a heavy sigh, regret still raw inside him over all of his mistakes where Hannah was concerned.

The only thing he could do was begin trying to fix them, one-by-one.

He picked up his phone and called the number on the pizza receipt.

"Hello?" the middle-aged builder answered.

"Hey, Paul. It's Gabe Lawson."

"Yeah, sure. How're you doing, Gabe?"

"I've been better," he admitted.

"I'll bet," Paul replied. "Had a feeling I might be hearing from you. Folks at the coffee shop this morning mentioned that you took a pretty bad tumble over at the Taylor place."

Gabe frowned. "It just happened last night. You mean to tell me people are talking about it already?"

Paul chuckled. "It's a small town. Word travels fast around here."

"No kidding." Gabe groaned, because it hurt too much to laugh. He supposed he'd better get used to the idea of small-town gossip, even if he was at the center of it. "Any chance your offer to lend a hand on the beach house is still open?"

"I've got a few commitments I'll need to shuffle, but sure, I can make the time to finish things up for you. Tell me what you need and I'll get right on it."

As Gabe went over the open items on the inspector's report with him, he couldn't help but reflect on the kindness he'd found in every corner of Crestpoint Beach since he'd arrived. He was still an outsider, having only been in town for roughly two months, yet he had never felt like a stranger.

For most of his life, Denver had been home. Until Wyatt's betrayal, Gabe never would have considered leaving his mountains for anywhere else. Now, he couldn't imagine going back to the hustle and anonymity of city life.

"Thanks, Paul," he said as they were wrapping up their call. "I really appreciate this."

"No problem. Happy to help."

Gabe set his phone down, his gaze drawn back to the delicate coquina shell.

He may have corrected course on the beach house, but eventually he would have to find a way to fix everything he'd done wrong with Hannah, too.

He only hoped she would give him the chance.

CHAPTER 15

Hannah called in sick at the Gift Emporium the day after Gabe's accident. And the day after that.

She hadn't missed a scheduled shift in any of the years she'd been working there, yet her guilt about leaving the store short-handed clung to her as she shuffled through the kitchen at nearly noon in her pajamas and flip-flops for the second day in a row.

Her sulk wasn't doing her any good. Nor was it making the hours since she last saw Gabe at the hospital any more bearable.

The truth was, she missed him.

Her father's advice to give Gabe space to heal and come around to forgiving her for pushing him into a reckless stunt had been well-meaning, but Hannah was about at her wits' end with being patient.

She loved Gabe, and nothing seemed right knowing he was only about a quarter of a mile up the beach at his cottage, yet she didn't feel welcome to walk over and see how he was doing. She had thought about calling him or texting, but every time she picked up her phone to reach out, she relived the memory of his pained face in the emergency room as he'd told her to leave.

As far as she knew, he hadn't even come to the beach house since he'd been home from the hospital.

Hannah couldn't explain her depth of sadness over the fact that he wasn't over there right now pounding, measuring, or sanding something. Instead, he'd sent another man to finish the work he could no longer do.

Yesterday afternoon, Hannah had walked past the house and spotted a local contractor, Paul Shubert, installing the new exterior locks the inspector had required. When the middle-aged man with the thick midsection and thin combover had waved to her in friendly greeting, Hannah had actually burst out in tears right on the spot.

She needed to pull herself together.

Either she was going to work up her nerve and tell Gabe Lawson exactly how she felt about this intolerable gulf between them and pray he felt the same way, or her heart was just going to have to find a way to beat without him.

At the moment, she didn't feel prepared to confront either of those plans. What she really needed was some advice from the one person she'd always turned to for comfort, support, and wisdom.

Slumping into one of the dining table chairs, she picked up her phone and dialed Annie.

"Hey, Banana. I've been thinking about you all morning. How are you holding up, honey?"

Her sister's voice was a calming sound that drew a heavy sigh from Hannah's lips.

"Uh, oh," Annie said. "That bad, huh?"

"Are you busy right now?"

"Not too busy for you." There was a slight pause on the other end of the line. "Don't tell me you're staying home sick again today?"

"Yes, and I can't stand my own miserable company for another minute." Hannah tilted her head back and closed her eyes. "I need someone else's voice in my head instead of mine for a little while."

"Sounds like you need more than that," Annie replied, a note of concern in her tone. "How about some chocolate therapy? Want to continue this conversation at Sweet on You?"

"Chocolate *and* cupcakes?" Hannah immediately perked up. "That's the best idea I've heard all day."

"I thought you might say that." Annie's smile colored her voice. "Now, go get out of your pajamas, take a nice hot shower, and I'll be at the house in twenty minutes to pick you up."

"Okay." Hannah paused. "Wait. How did you know I was still in my pajamas?"

Annie laughed. "Because you're my sister and I love you. I'll see you soon."

Hannah hung up, then hurried to get herself ready. Since she'd made the effort to clean up and blow dry her hair, she decided to go all out, forgoing her usual shorts and T-shirt for one of her lightweight dresses and a pair of flat sandals.

Annie rolled into the driveway just as expected. She arched her brows as Hannah opened the Corolla's passenger door and slid inside. "Look at you. Seems like you're feeling better already."

"Well, someone *did* promise me chocolate."

"Good point." Annie smiled. "Let's go see what's on today's cupcake menu."

They made the short drive to Sweet on You, the cute little

bakery in the center of town. The shop had been open for less than a year, but its proprietor, Jessica Summers, was already making a name for herself. Neither the locals nor the tourists who packed the place on any given day seemed able to get enough of her decadent cupcake creations.

Hannah and Annie were no exceptions.

The bell on the door gave a bright jingle announcing their entry to the cheery bakery. Inside, the scent of vanilla, cocoa, and buttercream filled the air. Hannah inhaled deeply, unable to keep the pleasure off her face at the comforting aromas. Next time she was feeling sorry for herself, she had to remember to stop in at Sweet on You and simply breathe.

The shop had the look of an old-fashioned ice cream parlor. In front were six small white wrought-iron tables, each with two chairs. Brass-trimmed, gleaming glass cases ran along one side of the store, displaying the vast assortment of fresh-baked, artfully decorated cupcakes for sale. A chalkboard stood near the entryway with the day's offerings written in pastel colors on the dark slate and accented with hand-drawn flourishes.

"Hey, Hannah. Hi, Annie." From behind the busy counter near the register, the strawberry-blonde proprietor glanced up and nodded to them in greeting as she tied a length of pink-and-white twine around a box of cupcakes and handed it to a customer.

Jessica Summers was about Hannah's age, always ready with a sunny smile and a friendly hello for everyone who came into her shop. Hannah had been a frequent customer from the time Sweet on You first opened, and she'd since gotten Annie hooked on the delicious confections, too.

"Ooh, Hannah, look at these double-fudge turtle

cupcakes." Annie pointed to one of the trays inside the glass case. "Look at all of that caramel."

Hannah peered at the mouthwatering assortment and couldn't contain her soft moan. "I'm definitely going to need one of those. And one of the chocolate-with-coconut-creams, too. Maybe I should ask Jessica to box up a dozen."

Annie slanted her a sympathetic look. "Let's start with one of each and a cappuccino. That ought to be enough sugar and caffeine to make you feel a little better. At least, for starters."

Hannah smiled in spite of her hurting heart. "I may still bring home a box of them. You know, for backup."

Jessica had finished up with the other customers and walked toward Hannah and Annie from the other side of the case. "What looks good today, ladies?"

"Everything," they both answered at the same time.

Hannah pointed to the turtle-inspired cupcake. "Does that one come in extra-large size?"

Jessica laughed. "That would technically be a cake, and, yes, I could make a custom one for you with a day's notice. I actually just had a request today for a double-fudge turtle wedding cake."

Annie's eyes widened. "I didn't know you made wedding cakes."

"I don't. That is, I hadn't really considered adding cakes of any kind to the shop, but I've been getting a quite a few inquiries, so maybe I should give it more thought."

"You definitely should," Annie agreed. "I doubt I'd have to twist my fiancé's arm to have one of your creations at our wedding."

Hannah glanced at her sister. "I thought you and Noah haven't set a date yet."

"We haven't, but that doesn't mean I'm not making a few

plans ahead of time." Annie smiled, then looked at Jessica. "Will you let me know if you do start offering wedding cakes?"

"Of course! What can I get for you both in the meantime?"

They made their selections and requested two cappuccinos. When their order was ready, Hannah grabbed an empty table for them near the shop's front window.

She dived right in, plunging her fork into the turtle cupcake first, then alternating to the chocolate-coconut. "Mmm," she sighed. "So. Good."

Annie nodded, licking her lips as she finished her first bite of a pretty chocolate-raspberry confection that had striped frosting and a lacey accent made of spun sugar. "They're almost too pretty to eat, aren't they?"

Hannah grinned. "Almost."

She shoveled in another big bite, following it with a sip of her cappuccino. While her senses were blissfully overloading on the sweets and coffee, there was no soothing the ache that sat like a cold lump of stone in the center of her chest.

"It's been two days, Annie."

"He still hasn't spoken to you?"

Hannah shook her head and stared down at the foam in her cup. "I never should've gone to the house that night. I should have just let him work in peace like he wanted to, but no...I had to go and ruin everything by inviting him up to the roof with me and nearly getting him killed."

"Gabe's a grown man, Hannah. You're not responsible for his decisions. If he went up there on the roof with you, that's exactly where he wanted to be."

Hannah wanted to believe that, but she was still miserable with guilt and regret. "You should've seen the pain he was in after he fell, Annie. He tried not to show it, but I could tell he was in agony. All because of me. He must hate me."

Annie's expression was soft with sympathy. "I'm sure he doesn't hate you, Hannah. The way things were going between you two, I'd say what he feels for you is quite the opposite."

Hannah had thought so, too. She and Gabe had gone so quickly from friction to friendly to falling in love, it had seemed like a wonderful dream. Now, she was left wondering if the feelings she thought Gabe had for her were only an illusion. Or, worse, they had been real...until the moment he'd tumbled off that roof.

"The one thing that matters the most to Gabe is his work. Rebuilding his company, proving to himself that he can do it on his own, after what happened with his partner. Those things are important to him, Annie."

"I'm sure they are," she answered gently. "But do you really think they're more important to him than you are?"

Hannah's heart didn't want to believe that, but each day that passed without hearing from him or seeing him made her hopes fade a little more. And she had to admit, as sad as she was over the past couple of days with no word from him, she was also starting to get angry.

While she was sulking in her pajamas and eating her feelings, had Gabe even given her a moment's thought? Didn't he miss her the way she was missing him? She felt as though a piece of her was gone. Hannah absently reached up to her throat to touch the sweet coquina shell necklace he'd made for her, but even that was lost now.

Frowning, she stabbed her fork into the last bite of her double-fudge cupcake.

"If Gabe does care about me even a little bit, why hasn't he tried to call me? Why hasn't he come around to see me? At least I know he's alive, because he sent Paul Shubert out to finish the beach house in his place." Hannah scoffed quietly. "I suppose I should be grateful for that, right? It looks like we're going to make the inspection, after all."

"That is good news," Annie said. "I never doubted that Gabe would see us through to the end, just like he'd promised."

Hannah had never doubted that, either. Gabe's work ethic was impeccable. So was his honor. Who else would personally pay back the debts racked up by a thieving business partner?

Knowing those things about him only made it harder to accept that he could evidently shut her out of his heart and walk away.

He wasn't a quitter. Except, evidently, when it came to her.

Well, maybe Gabe Lawson didn't realize it, but Hannah wasn't a quitter, either.

A sense of resolve galvanized her as she picked up her cappuccino and drained the cup. Maybe it was the sugar and caffeine coursing through her system giving her the courage she hadn't felt until now. Whatever it was, she seized on it.

"Annie, I have to go."

"Go?" Her sister stared at her in confusion. "Go where?"

"To Gabe's house."

Annie gaped. "Now?"

"Yes, now. I should have done this two days ago." Hannah stood up. "I love him, Annie. I think I've been in love with Gabe from the minute he stepped up onto the veranda at nine o'clock that first morning. On the dot," she added, smiling in spite of herself. "So, if he doesn't want me in his life, then he's going to have to say it to my face."

CHAPTER 16

"You want to grab the other end of that two-by-eight for me, Henry?"

Gabe stood with his friend in the lumber supply warehouse a couple of towns over from Crestpoint Beach. All around them was the whirr of circular saws and the intermittent beeps and whines of construction equipment while contractors and workmen went about their business.

These were his people, his natural habitat. This was where Gabe had always felt most at home, yet nothing felt right anymore.

It wasn't only because of the injury that still had his right arm out of commission in its sling.

It was mostly because it had been two days since he'd last seen or spoken to Hannah.

"Not that two-by-eight," he snapped impatiently at Henry, gesturing with his left hand to a smooth piece of oak hardwood next to the one in his friend's hands. "This one right here."

Henry sent a beleaguered look at him. "What's the difference, man? You've gone through the whole stack. All of these boards look the same to me."

Gabe scowled. "It has to be perfect."

"Fine, whatever you say." Shrugging, Henry picked up the end of the one Gabe pointed to. "What are we doing with this, anyway?"

"We're going to have them cut it for me."

They carried the plank over to the saws and Gabe gave the measurements to the operator working the equipment. Ordinarily, he would have trimmed the piece himself to make sure it was exactly how he wanted it, but with his bum arm, he had to rely on others.

He wasn't even able to drive himself now that he couldn't use his right hand to shift gears. Thankfully, Henry had the afternoon off and had been willing to shuttle him around on today's couple of errands.

"Precisely those measurements," Gabe ordered the man at the machine.

When he glanced back at Henry, he was met with his friend's questioning look.

Gabe felt his brow furrow deeper. "What's wrong?"

"That's what I was going to ask you. You've been bristly since you called to ask me to shuttle you around town today. Are you skipping your pain meds or something?"

"I don't need pain medicine," Gabe replied tersely. "My arm is fine. Rather, it will be…in about three more months."

"So, if it's not your arm that's bothering you, then it must be something else. Your heart, maybe?" Henry let go of a sigh. "Seriously, Gabe. Are you okay?"

It was hard for him to lie, especially to someone who had known him for years. Despite the extended period of time when he and Henry had lived multiple states away from each other, that hadn't changed his friend's ability to see right through him.

Was he okay? Gabe had been trying to pretend he was, but he wasn't even fooling himself. He swallowed and shook his head. "Not really," he admitted quietly.

"You really fell hard for Hannah, didn't you?"

"Yeah. I didn't plan to, but I did."

Henry lightly cuffed him on his good shoulder. "You can't plan for everything, man. Especially love. It doesn't come with a blueprint or a measuring tape. It just happens. Usually at the worst possible time, with the worst possible woman."

That kind of insight from his free-wheeling, serially single friend was unexpected. The semi-revelation that Henry may be hiding his own broken heart came as a surprise, too.

Gabe stared at him. "When did you get so wise when it comes to relationships? What happened to 'my true love is adrenaline'?"

Chuckling, Henry held up his hands. "Hey, we're not talking about me right now. Don't try to change the subject."

"All right, but don't think I'm going to forget to bring this up with you again later."

"Fair enough." Henry studied him. "Why don't you just pick up the phone and call her, Gabe? It's obvious to me and anyone else looking at your hangdog face right now that you're miserable without Hannah."

Gabe couldn't deny it. He was miserable. He'd let his guilt and self-directed anger push Hannah away, and now he was afraid she might never come back.

He had wanted to call her and apologize. In fact, he'd started to make that call many times, especially the first day he was home. Every time, he disconnected before he'd dialed her whole number. As the hours since his release from the hospital had lengthened and then eventually two full days had passed, he no longer knew how to say everything he wanted to say to Hannah.

He was sorry.

He missed her.

He needed her.

He loved her.

Hannah deserved to hear all of those truths and more. He just had to find a way to make her listen.

Paul's work on the beach house was coming along well, but it would still be another day or two before everything was completed. Gabe intended to head over today to check in on the progress.

He also had something he wanted to take care of personally while he was there.

The workman finished cutting and smoothing the oak plank and stepped back to let Gabe take a look. He measured the thirty-six-inch length and nodded.

Henry held up the pair of triangle-cut oak supports they'd picked up from another area of the wood shop. "What are you making, a bookshelf?"

Gabe smirked and shook his head. "It's an apology. One I hope I'm not too late to deliver."

He had another piece of that apology in his pocket. He shouldn't have waited until now to let Hannah know what she meant to him.

After two days and counting since he'd seen her or talked to her, he knew one thing for sure: he never wanted to go this long without Hannah beside him ever again.

The pain in his shoulder was temporary. It was a setback to his business, but it wasn't permanent. It wouldn't last, not like his feelings for Hannah.

What he felt for her was forever.

He'd made a lot of colossal mistakes in his life, but the worst was pushing away the one woman he couldn't live without. He hoped she could forgive him for that. If she couldn't, he would never forgive himself.

Carrying the finished length of oak in his good hand, he set it on the wheeled cart with the rest of the items.

"All right," he said to Henry. "I have everything I need to get started."

"Great. Where are we off to next?"

"The beach house. There's something there that I need to take care of before anything else."

CHAPTER 17

He wasn't home.

Hannah rapped on the cottage door again and waited. No sounds or movement came from inside, even though Gabe's truck was parked in the short driveway. He probably couldn't drive it until his shoulder was healed.

Maybe she should have called first, if for no other reason than to make sure he would actually be there before she told Annie to drop her off and leave.

Hannah had never dropped in at his place unannounced before, but she had felt the need to act while she still had her nerve. An anxious part of her worried that if she had called him beforehand, it might only have given him the opportunity to tell her to stay away.

By stopping in to see him, she was still running the risk of getting her heart stomped on, but it had seemed a lot better than another day or hour or minute of not knowing if there was anything left between them. Or if there ever had been.

She sighed, feeling like a fool as she stood on the small, covered porch alone. Thankfully, the only witnesses to her awkwardness were the pelicans and seagulls flying over the water hunting for fish just off the beach.

Deflated, Hannah pivoted away from the door. So much for her grand plan to take matters into her own hands with Gabe. Even her sugar-and-caffeine-enhanced courage was starting to abandon her.

There was nothing left for her to do now but turn around and walk back home.

Slipping out of her sandals, she hooked her finger through the straps and stepped off the porch into the sand. The way her heart felt so heavy in her chest, the fifteen-minute walk started to feel like an hour.

She passed a few local couples on their daily strolls, most of them holding hands or chatting together as they stepped past her. Several families had set up camp on the beach with colorful umbrellas and blankets while enjoying the beautiful day with their squealing, delighted kids.

Hannah offered everyone smiles and friendly waves, but she was only going through the motions.

She wanted some of their happiness, too. She wanted the joy and comfort of a family—one of her own, that she could share with a partner who made her feel loved and understood and excited simply to be alive.

The way she felt when she was with Gabe.

What was she going to do if the only man she ever wanted was the one she could never have?

Hannah's shoulders slumped as she drew nearer to the beach house. The metallic whine of a drill echoed over the steady rhythm of the waves and the ocean breeze. Hearing it was just another reminder of Gabe's absence.

Maybe she should have been more excited to know the work on the house was not only continuing but reaching completion. She and Annie had already scheduled the next inspection date for the end of the week, and they had no doubts that Jane Peavey would find nothing to peer at disapprovingly over her red-framed glasses this time.

Gabe's work had been meticulous and well-planned out, and his replacement was finishing up the remaining tasks with ease.

As Hannah walked closer to the beautiful Victorian, some of her sadness did fade a little. She couldn't help but feel an overwhelming sense of pride at what she and Annie had accomplished together. The house had never looked more inviting, nor more loved.

Thanks to their shared vision and Gabe's exacting attention to detail, the large blue-and-white house gleamed like a jewel in the sunlight.

Hannah could hardly wait until she and Annie welcomed their first guests.

She drifted closer, frowning when she realized there was a man on the roof. Crouched on one knee, he was hunched over with a drill in his hand, working on something under the window of the second-floor bedroom.

It wasn't Paul Shubert—of that much, she was certain.

No, this man was much younger and leaner. His muscular frame and coffee-dark hair made every cell in Hannah's body light up with recognition.

Impossible recognition.

What on earth would Gabe be doing working at the house?

Not just that…what was he doing on the roof?

Hannah's heart started thumping heavily in her chest. She didn't know if she should call out to him or not. The last thing she wanted to do was startle him into another perilous fall.

She picked up her pace, disbelief coursing through her as she neared the veranda steps and confirmed that it really was him up there. He aimed the drill down at the rooftop and the high-pitched whine filled the air again.

Hannah's bare feet carried her silently into the house and up the stairs. By the time she entered the bedroom where she had painted her stargazer mural, her heart had climbed all the way up into her throat in a mix of confusion, curiosity…and hope.

The window was open, bringing in the warm air and the spicy scent of the man she would know anywhere. Hannah set her sandals down on the floor and moved cautiously forward.

"Gabe?" She breathed out quietly, part of her still unsure she could trust her senses.

He lifted his head and spotted her inside the room. His expression registered surprise, but she couldn't tell anything more from the steady gaze that was locked on her now.

She noticed his right arm was out of its sling, though he was using it carefully.

Hannah frowned, folding her arms in front of her as she went to the opened window. "What are you doing here? You should be home, resting."

"I realized there was something I needed to do, and it couldn't wait."

Concern gripped her as his terrifying fall a few nights ago repeated in her mind. "You shouldn't be up there, Gabe. Couldn't Paul fix whatever you're doing?"

"Not this," he said.

She glanced around, realizing how quiet the house was now. "Where is Paul, anyway?"

"I sent him home for the day."

"Why? What exactly are you working on?"

He looked so serious, she could hardly contain the anxious pound of her heartbeat as she stared at him.

Then he extended his hand toward her. "Would you like to see?"

She gave him a nod and placed her fingers in his palm.

Hannah didn't need assistance to climb out of the window and onto the roof, but she allowed herself to revel in the brief contact anyway. His strong fingers closed around her hand, gently supporting her as she stepped over the sill.

He crouched in front of a small bench seat made of smooth wood, which he had securely fastened to the roof.

"Now, anyone can watch the stars without risking a fall."

Hannah glanced from him to the seat that was just large enough for two if they huddled close. It wasn't fancy or elaborately made, but she had never seen anything so beautiful in her life.

"You made this?"

His smile was as sheepish as his shrug. "I had some help. It's not my best work, but I'll make you a better one once my arm is healed."

"No." Hannah slowly shook her head. "I don't want you to change a thing. It's perfect, Gabe."

It took all her effort not to throw her arms around him right on the spot. If they hadn't been perched on the sloped roof again, she doubted she would've been able to keep her emotions under control.

Plus, she was confused. After two days without a word from him, was she reading too much into his thoughtful gesture?

Was she reading too much into the tender earnestness of his gaze?

"Gabe, I'm sorry about what happened to you. I'm sorry I

made you come up here with me that night. I never should have—"

"No," he said gently, shaking his head. "You have nothing to apologize for, Hannah."

She drew in a breath. "But your arm—"

"Will heal," he interjected calmly.

She frowned. "Gabe, your work…all of your plans for starting your business—"

"It will all be waiting for me when I'm ready to go back to it, Hannah." Doubt flickered in his normally confident green eyes. "The only thing I'm afraid might not be there anymore is you."

Shock made her voice dry up. She could hardly breathe for the hope that surged inside her as he spoke. Gabe shifted his position, moving up onto the bench while guiding her down beside him at the same time. She sat tentatively, her heart on the verge of exploding with joy as he took her hand in his.

"I've been miserable these past couple of days, Hannah. Not because of my injuries, but because of you. Because you're the best thing that's ever happened to me, and that night I realized how quickly I could've lost you. If it had been you who fell off this roof…" His words faded and he blew out a terse breath. "That's all I could think about when I was lying in the ER. What if you had been hurt instead of me? I wouldn't have been able to handle that kind of loss, Hannah. I couldn't even deal with the thought of it that night, so I pushed you away when all I really wanted was to hold you close and never let go."

She smiled, swallowing on her constricted throat. "So, you thought you'd climb up here by yourself with your one good arm and make a bench for stargazing?"

His mouth quirked, but his gaze burned with solemnness.

"That was the plan, yes. And once I had this little bench installed, I was going to climb back down and go look for you."

She drew in a shallow breath. "You were?"

He nodded.

"What were you going to say when you found me?"

He swiveled so he was facing her, then lifted his hand to lightly stroke her cheek. "What I was going to say to you, my sweet, beautiful Hannah, is that I'm sorry. That I've missed you more than you can possibly know these past couple of days."

"Oh, Gabe," she whispered. "I've missed you, too."

A tear spilled over and slid down her cheek. He caught it with his thumb, gently wiping it away. His gaze held hers with unwavering resolve. "I was going tell you that you're the most important thing in my life, Hannah, and that I don't ever want to be without you again…because I love you."

"You do?"

His mouth curved in a tender smile. "From the moment I first saw you on the veranda down there. You were the burst of color and light and pure joy I never realized I was missing. You've been that for me since the moment we met."

A happy sob burst out of her. She wanted to speak, but his words kept knocking the breath from her and making her heart swell with such intense emotion it was hard to find her voice.

A pensive look crossed his face and he moved back a little. "I have something that belongs to you."

Reaching into the pocket of his shorts, he withdrew the coquina shell necklace he'd made for her. Except now the bakery twine had been replaced with a gleaming gold chain.

"I thought I lost this that night. Gabe, where did you find it?"

"I had the shell in my hand when I hit the sand. It was still there, curled in my fist in the ER, when the doctor reset my shoulder." He gave a mild shrug. "I kept it because it really belongs to you, and I wanted to be able to give it back to you."

Hannah swallowed as he unfastened the clasp and held both ends in his hands.

"May I?" he asked.

She gave a shaky nod. The warmth and scent of him as he leaned forward made her dizzy, but in the best way. She waited, unable to breathe as he reached around to the back of her neck and secured the chain.

Hannah reached up to touch the delicate shell where it now rested above her heart. "I can't believe you fixed this for me."

He drew back from her, his eyes filled with deep affection...and a trace of uncertainty. "I can fix your house and your necklace, Hannah...but what I really want to know is can I fix things between us?"

"You already have." She stifled a giddy laugh. "Before I came here, I was at your cottage. I went there because I was going to tell you everything you just told me."

He exhaled as if he'd been holding his breath waiting for her reply. A smile broke over his handsome face and he leaned forward, their lips meeting in a tender, yet powerful kiss.

It had only been days since she'd felt his mouth on hers, yet it had felt like an eternity until now. Hannah pushed her hand up into his hair as he grabbed her around the waist with his good arm and pulled her closer to him on the bench and kissed her more deeply.

When they paused to catch their breath, Hannah brought

her hands up to his face and cradled his firm jaw. Her heart overflowed with all of the feelings she had for this man.

Her man.

"I've missed you so much," she murmured, her voice breaking with emotion. "And I love you, too. I'm going to love you forever, Gabe Lawson."

A grin tugged at the edge of his lips. "I sure like the sound of that."

"Good, because you're going to be hearing it a lot from now on. I love you."

"I love you, too." He smiled as he rested his forehead against hers, yet his voice had never sounded more solemn. "I can't wait to start forever with you, Hannah."

She could hardly contain all of the joy and devotion that soared to life inside her. "Then let's begin right now, with another kiss."

He laughed, gathering her into his arms and kissing her under the warmth of a clear blue sky and a future that was bright with hope, shared dreams, and love.

EPILOGUE

Two weeks later, Hannah stood anxiously next to Annie as the inspector walked out of the first-floor bedroom, clipboard in her hand.

It was the final room in the beach house to be reviewed. The final hurdle to be cleared before Ms. Peavey either signed her approval on her report, or delayed the B&B's opening with another round of fixes to be addressed.

Her low heels clopped on the hardwood as she walked out to the living room to rejoin the sisters. Hannah held her breath as the woman peered at them over the rims of her red glasses.

"All right, I believe I have everything I need."

Bracing the clipboard against her hip, she pulled a pen from behind her ear and scribbled her name at the bottom of the paper. Then she tore off the top sheet and held it out to them.

Hannah's tension was ratcheted so high, she couldn't stop herself from grabbing it first. Her eyes immediately drifted to the signature line.

"Approved." She glanced at Annie, a smile breaking across her face. "We're approved!"

"We are?" Hannah showed her the report and Annie let out an excited cry. "We are! Ms. Peavey, thank you very much."

The inspector smiled as Annie shook her hand. Hannah reached out next, then shot forward and gave the older woman a hug, simply because she couldn't contain her joy.

"Oh!" Ms. Peavey said as she was briefly pulled into Hannah's arms. When she stepped back, she laughed awkwardly. "All right, then. I'm glad everything worked out. You have a truly beautiful guest house here. All of the finishing touches and repairs I requested are beyond my expectations."

Hannah beamed with pride at the praise, not only for Annie and herself, but for Gabe's work on the house as well.

"Thank you again," Annie said. "We hope our B&B will add to the charm and hospitality of Crestpoint Beach."

Ms. Peavey nodded. "I'm sure it will. I may even have to book a little getaway here for myself one day."

Hannah laughed. "We'd love to have you."

"Very well," the woman replied, tucking the clipboard under her arm. "I should leave you to celebrate the good news. It looks like you've got a few folks waiting outside to hear the verdict."

Hannah and Annie exchanged a smile as they walked Ms. Peavey out to the veranda. Gathered on the beach was the group of people she'd mentioned. Hannah could hardly contain her excitement as she glanced out at her family and friends.

They all had assembled for a picnic lunch, and to either cheer on their success or commiserate if this new inspection had ended in disappointment or setbacks.

Hannah's gaze searched out Gabe among the small crowd. As soon as he saw her, he paused in conversation with her father.

Noah waited outside for Annie, too, along with Lainey and her boyfriend, Mason. Even Zoe and Henry had come out to offer their moral support.

"Congratulations again on your beautiful house," Ms. Peavey said. "And good luck with your business. You've got something really special here."

After repeating their thanks and saying goodbye, the sisters watched as the inspector stepped down the sturdy new steps Gabe had built and walked around to her car.

As soon as she was gone, Hannah turned to Annie and threw her arms around her. "We did it. We actually did it, Annie!"

"I know. I can hardly believe it." They laughed together as they hugged. When they pulled apart, Annie's eyes glistened with emotion. "I'm so proud to be your sister, and I can't wait to officially become your business partner, too."

"I feel the same way," Hannah replied, feeling fortunate and grateful to have Annie back in her life again. The fact that they would soon be opening their grandparents' home to people in Crestpoint Beach and around the world only made her more cognizant of all the blessings she had been gifted with throughout her life.

Now, she had Gabe to add to that list, too.

"I guess we should go deliver the good news, right?"

Annie nodded. "Let's go."

With the inspector's report clutched in one hand and her sister's fingers linked through her other, Hannah hopped off the veranda steps onto the beach.

"It's approved!" Hannah shouted.

Hoots of jubilation and happy applause answered her announcement. Gabe and Noah broke from the group to meet Hannah and Annie halfway across the sand. Gabe's arm was still in its sling, so as much as she wanted to leap into his embrace, Hannah carefully wrapped her arms around him and rested her cheek against his chest.

Annie and Noah embraced beside them, murmuring quiet words meant only for each other.

Hannah soaked everything in, content in the moment. She didn't think her heart could contain all of the happiness it held, then Gabe tipped her face up on his fingertips and met her lips with his.

"Congratulations, sweetheart."

"Thank you." She smiled up at him, certain she must be glowing with elation…and love. "None of this would be possible without you, Gabe."

He scowled in disagreement, and she almost laughed at the way his furrowed brow only endeared him to her all the more now.

"Whatever I did on the house was nothing compared to what you and Annie have accomplished together. The two of you deserve all of the credit Hannah. I'm just pleased to be able to see you this happy."

She reached up and brushed her fingers through his dark hair. "Thank you for saying that. What I really meant was, none of this would be possible without you, because if you weren't in my life, I wouldn't be feeling half the joy I am now. Having you beside me makes everything more meaningful."

His answering smile kindled a warmth in her soul. "Do you have any idea how much I love you?"

She laughed softly. "If it's half as much as I love you, I can't ask for any more."

He bent his head down and slowly kissed her, right in front of her father and everyone. Then he took the inspector's report out of her hand and tucked the folded paper into his back pocket. "Come on. I guess I can't keep you all to myself all day, as much as I'd like to."

With Gabe's arm draped around her shoulders, they walked back to join the rest of their family and friends. Annie and Noah followed as well.

As the two couples arrived near the blankets and the waiting food, Frank Taylor was the first to speak.

"Congratulations," he said, beaming at his daughters.

"Thanks, Dad." Hannah said, with Annie echoing her reply.

He smiled at them the way he did so often when they were kids, his blue eyes full of affection, and his kind face soft with pride.

"I've always been proud of you two girls, but today means more to me than either of you could possibly know. Seeing you work together to bring this house back to life has made me realize how extraordinary you both are—individually, and also as a team. You're both so gifted, but in different ways. This house is a reflection of both of you now. It's beautiful and resilient, just like my two daughters."

Hannah glanced at Annie and found her sister looking at her, too. They had always been close, even during the years Annie was gone.

Now, their bond was stronger than ever.

They would always be sisters, but over the past few months they had also become best friends. They had the beach house to thank for that. Soon, they would open their doors to the public. Hannah hoped the bed-and-breakfast would bring some of the same magic to their guests that it had given to Annie and her.

And to their father.

They stepped forward in unison to embrace their dad. His strong arms encircled them, too, holding them tight.

It felt good to Hannah to have her family together again.

It felt even better to count Gabe among her family, too.

As she moved out of her father's embrace, she couldn't help noticing the look of hesitation on his face.

"What is it, Dad?"

"There seems to be one thing you girls have forgotten to do."

She and Annie looked at each other in confusion. "We have?"

Frank Taylor nodded. "What are you going to name the place?"

"Oh." He was right. They had been so consumed with the renovations and all of the other bumps along the way, they hadn't talked about what to call the B&B once it was finished.

Annie shrugged. "I guess we'd better come up with something if we want to start advertising for our first guests."

Hannah frowned. "It has to be something special."

Their father cleared his throat. "Would you allow an old man to offer a suggestion?"

"Of course," they both said.

Smiling fondly at them, he reached out and took Annie's hand in one of his, and Hannah's in the other. "I've watched both of you grow and thrive over these past few months. Things haven't been easy for either of you, I know. You've faced your troubles and heartbreaks, but you've also been blessed with many moments of joy along the way. That's how life is, don't you agree? The tide gets low sometimes, but you can always count on the fact that it will rise again. It keeps turning, just like life. There is always an opportunity for a fresh start or a new beginning, even when we least expect it."

"That's true," Hannah said, glancing at Gabe.

Annie sent a loving look at Noah. "Sometimes, if we're really lucky we get second chances, too."

Frank Taylor nodded. "It occurs to me that not only the both of you but this house, too, have been given a fresh start. A turn in the tide." He smiled as he said it. "Seems to me that's about as fitting a name as any for everything you're building together. All of you," he added, including Gabe and Noah in his warm smile.

"Turning Tides," Hannah said, swiping at her misting eyes. "What do you think, Annie?"

Her sister's blue gaze was swimming with tears, too. "I love it."

Hannah nodded. "So do I."

Gabe and Noah both grinned in approval.

"Well, that settles it," Frank Taylor said. "To the Turning Tides B&B!"

Cheers went up from everyone in response. The sound of a champagne cork popping punctuated the laughs and excitement, and in moments Henry had poured everyone a small toast in red plastic cups.

They gathered on the blankets to serve the food and continue their celebration. As they ate and talked and laughed, Zoe announced that she was gifting the newly christened B&B a pair of handcrafted rocking chairs she'd made for the veranda.

It was a perfect day, shared with the people Hannah loved the most.

After the well-wishes and congratulations were over, Gabe drew her aside to walk along the water's edge with him. Hannah leaned against him, her arm circled around his back.

"I can't believe it's really happening, Gabe. Annie and I will be opening our B&B in time for the summer season. Shouldn't I be panicking about that or something? We've never done anything like this before. Maybe I should be terrified, but all I feel is excitement."

"You're going to be great." He hugged her close. "I love seeing you this happy."

Hannah slowed her pace, until they had both paused in the sand. The warm waves lapped against their feet and ankles. "I've never been happier in my life."

"Neither have I." He smiled at her, love shining in his gaze.

He seemed in no hurry to resume walking or to rejoin their family and friends back on the beach. With a gentle touch, he smoothed his fingers over her cheek as some of her loose hair caught on the breeze.

When Gabe was looking at her like that, Hannah was content never to move again.

His caress drifted tenderly over her face. "For as long as I can remember, whenever I thought of home, I pictured the mountains where I grew up. I never imagined I would leave. I didn't think there'd be anything worth seeing or having in any other place in the world. Then life sent me here."

Hannah smiled, recalling how he'd struggled to get acclimated to flat land and a sweltering Florida sun. He still preferred his subdued colors, but she couldn't help feeling a personal sense of accomplishment that today he was actually wearing one of the short-sleeved tropical shirts she'd brought home from the Emporium for him as a joke the other day.

He caressed her face, smirking as if he knew what she was thinking. "Everything here was so different from what I was used to. Including you."

"Total opposites," she agreed. "For example, I love ABBA, and you…well, lucky for you, I was willing to not to hold your lack of musical taste against you."

"Yes, lucky for me." His gaze grew solemn. "I never imagined I'd find another place where I truly felt I belonged. But I have now."

"You have?"

He nodded. "It's right here, Hannah. With you."

She stared up at his handsome face, seeing forever in his warm green eyes as he lowered his head and kissed her.

In the distance, were the sounds of joy and laughter coming from their family and friends, while all around her and Gabe as they embraced and whispered promises for their future together, the constant ebb and flow of the warm tide rolled gently against the sand.

THANK you so much for joining Hannah and Gabe on the journey to their happily-ever-after. I hope you loved this new visit to Crestpoint Beach!

If you enjoyed **Meant to Be**, please let me know by sharing your review for the book on Amazon, Goodreads, or BookBub.

Are you ready for the next book in the Turning Tides B&B series?

You've met Hannah and Annie's friend, furniture-maker

Zoe Wright, in the first two books. Now it's her turn to discover that love often happens when you least expect it. Come back to Crestpoint Beach with the newest novel in the series, **Maybe This Time**. Releasing in April 2021 and available for pre-order now!

WANT A MONTHLY CHANCE TO WIN A SIGNED BOOK?

JOIN MY READER LIST

Be sure to join my private email list at CarlyGrant.com to get updates on my new and upcoming books, as well as special sales and promotions, exclusive content, and more.

Each month, active subscribers also have a chance to win a signed paperback copy of Back to You!

TURNING TIDES SERIES

Back to You
Meant to Be
Maybe This Time
Sweet on You (coming soon)

ABOUT THE AUTHOR

Carly Grant loves Hallmark movies, small-town life, sandy beaches, kittens, and cupcakes--not necessarily in that order. She lives in her hometown in Florida with her husband, where she spends her days soaking up the sunshine and dreaming up sweet romances and happily-ever-afters.

Visit CarlyGrant.com for book info and more!

facebook.com/CarlyGrantAuthor
bookbub.com/profile/carly-grant
goodreads.com/carlygrantauthor

Made in the USA
Las Vegas, NV
31 March 2023

69957312R00104